WHERE TRADE WINDS MEET
By
L.J. Green

SWEET HISTORICAL ROMANCE FICTION

All rights reserved. Copyright © 2024 L.J. Green and Jolene MacFadden Kowalchuk

This is a work of fiction. Similarities to real people, places, or events are entirely coincidental or are referenced within the storyline as remembrance events and people of the past.
No part of this publication may be reproduced, distributed, or transmitted in any form or by any means, including photocopying, recording, or other electronic or mechanical methods, without the prior written permission of the publisher, except in the case of brief quotations embodied in critical reviews and certain other noncommercial uses permitted by copyright law. For permission requests, write to the publisher, addressed "Attention: Permissions Coordinator," at the address below.

WHERE TRADE WINDS MEET
Historical Fiction - Tropical Romance
Written by L.J. Green

Library of Congress Control No (LCCN): 2024923796
eBook ISBN: 978-1-961386-14-3
Paperback ISBN: 978-1-961386-15-0
Hardback ISBN: 978-1-961386-16-7
Audio ISBN: 978-1-961386-17-4
Southern Dragon Publishing
c/o Jolene MacFadden-Kowalchuk
PO Box 1712
Mayo, FL 32066
https://southerndragonpublishing.com

A Note To My Readers and Writers Friends at First Coast Romance Writers

First, I want to thank all my writing friends at the First Coast Romance Writer's group in Jacksonville, Florida who helped me get my first novella published, "Widow's Dilemma in Cuba" and now this second story. Both stories were published first in their Romancing the Tropics anthologies to help raise money for the group to promote writing excellence in North Florida. This current story has been expanded and re-edited to bring it almost to a full novel.

Check out their website:

https://FirstCoastRomanceWriters.com

They have encouraged me to continue my writing journey and get a new editor when my friend and writing mentor, Sydney Clary, passed away this past summer. She, more than anyone, encouraged me to begin my fiction writing journey. Such a talented lady who did not get a chance to tell all the stories she had living in her head.

Check out her website:

https://laceydancer.com

She may be gone, but she has left a wealth of reading enjoyment behind. We can only hope that her family re-publish all of her backlist very soon.

To My Readers:

I am a historian by heart and love to gather information about other times, places and people. I also believe that those who have passed before us can still contribute to our future by sharing their stories with each new generation. As writers, we have the ability to bring people who have long since passed back to life in the pages of our stories.

Each of the stories I write include the names, occupations and sometimes the descriptions of people who have lived and worked in the area my stories are set. I comb through all types of genealogy records and old newspapers and magazines to add background characters to my stories. This story, however, includes those who lived in Key West during the time I wrote about as main characters. The lineage of these characters has died out, but their lives, loves, hopes and dreams can be remembered.

I hope you enjoy this peak into another time and place.

PROLOGUE

"Many American children to the north are not as privileged to learn your rich history here in the tropical region of these United States. For our lessons this includes not only Key West and all its attached smaller keys but also Cuba and the Bahama islands. Your families originally came from England and Spain and have been moving about these parts since the early 1600s. They created plantations for sugar and cotton on the bigger islands. They held slaves and finally set them free, much sooner than did the United States. The British Empire still controls much of the Bahama islands even today. Now, in 1907, your descendants have become prominent merchants on the smaller islands as well as all along the keys. Your families are heavily involved in the government offices and finance too," Miss Anderson enthused.

"Oh, who cares about all those faraway people?" Albert Pinder said snidely.

He threw a paper wad into Muriel's hair. She was his betrothed. He had learned this when he overheard his father and Muriel's talking over drinks at The Wrecker's Bar last year. He was not sure what it meant but it sounded important. Curious to know what it meant the next day, while everyone was at recess, he had snuck into the classroom to look it up in Miss Anderson's *Webster's Dictionary*. That silly book was the teacher's prized possession, he snorted at that absurdity. He remembered she had ordered it by mail from New York City the previous year.

Finally, finding the word in the book, he read that *betrothed* meant that Muriel belonged to him. He puffed up his chest at that. When he asked his father about it the following week, Albert learned that he had to wait until they reached eighteen. He was unhappy about waiting, but he could do it. After all, they were both the same age, and it was only five years away.

Muriel felt something wet in her hair and pulled it from her pinned-up curls. Turning around, she threw it back at Albert. It had to be him. He was the only boy in class who picked on her this year. Mother said he was sweet on her. Her friends, Mabel and Frieda, said he was creepy, always lurking about. Muriel gave Albert an impatient look and mouthed, "Stop that."

Albert batted away the wet paper and gave Muriel what he thought was a seductive look.

Muriel saw the look. Harrumphing to herself she was not impressed with that smug, self-important expression. She found it disgusting and quickly turned back around to listen to what Miss Anderson was saying.

"Children, whatever is going on over there, please save it for recess." Miss Anderson cleared her throat and began again. "As I was saying, the families of Albury, Lowe, Parker, Pinder, Roberts, Russell, and Sweeting have inhabited Key West since the 1830s. The Conchs, as you are now called, have a proud seafaring tradition of sponging, wrecking, and serving on ships that travel these lovely blue waters. Some scholars have begun to record your language and history. That is why I came here.

WHERE TRADE WINDS MEET

I want to write a book about your history, traditions, and language. And I hope you will help me complete it."

Miss Anderson reminded the class that Key West had been a British loyalist stronghold, but after the United States won its independence, most loyalists fled back to the Bahamas. Some had returned prior to the Civil War but then fled back again to the other islands when the South lost. Those who stayed lived through various other types of invasions including the Cubans with their cigar businesses, the northerners coming down to make their mark and enjoy the tropical weather and, of course, Mother Nature, whose continuous storms raged through the area every year. But the Conchs stayed fast, incorporated some of traditions into their own culture, but still kept their relaxed attitude of, "What will be, will be" about most things in their lives. They instilled in their children pride of heritage, keeping those traditions, strong will, and to keep together.

The children were getting restless with all the talk. They did not understand why Miss Anderson wanted to record their lives, but they would help her. She respected their ways and had asked each of their parents to take part. She had volunteered to work with the various ladies' groups at each church whenever there were projects to complete. While Key West had several kinds of churches, there were more saloons. Both were needed by the temporary residents—seamen, restless rich people, and families moving through to other places.

Miss Anderson released the class to go outside, Muriel and her two friends went to sit in the shade of the old kapok tree. The bottom of the tree looked like it had been sliced and mushed into folds resembling a lady's skirt. Within the four folds, the girls had private sections where they could sit. Above, the limbs were intricately woven in a curving pattern and adorned with lush green leaves. Suddenly, Albert towered silently over the three girls who had been giggling and enjoying their free time. Not wanting to be at a disadvantage, all three girls popped up at once and stared him down.

Albert backed up, a little surprised at the girls' agility and coordinated response. Although they were all close in age, he was the man and would reign supreme over them. He asserted his dominance, informing Muriel, "Our fathers have agreed that we are betrothed."

"Albert, I do not know what you mean by that, but my father has said nothing to me."

"It means you belong to me once you and I turn eighteen." Jutting his chin, he smirked, daring her to dispute it.

Muriel's shock quickly turned into fury as she unleashed a punch to Albert's nose. "I am not anyone's possession!" she shouted, running back to the classroom.

Mabel and Frieda, shocked at the exchange, ran after her.

Albert picked himself up and looked around to make sure no one else had witnessed his humiliation. Since Muriel had drawn no blood, he went around the back of the building to splash water on his face and wash his hands at the pump. "She will get hers one day. When she is mine, I will tame that girl."

His eyes were dark pinpoints, and his expression scared a younger boy who quickly moved away from the water pump. The boy shivered and prayed that whoever the girl was, she would escape.

WHERE TRADE WINDS MEET

The next day Muriel confronted her father, "Sir, I have been told that I am betrothed to that Albert Pinder." She stood straight and defiant, but her tone was respectful.

"Yes, the Pinder family has been in Key West for generations," Charles Russell replied. "It is a suitable match."

"Sir, Albert Pinder is not a suitable match for anyone. He has a devil's streak in him." She shuddered as she spoke, hoping that her father would believe her and call it off.

"With my sister marrying into a Cuban family, there has been a discussion among our group that our family heritage is being diluted. The idea has been raised that marrying outside our community has caused us to lose our true Conch identity. Sons and daughters of high society British Bahamian plantation owners are sent back to England to find suitable matches. Regrettably, we do not possess that advantage. Our family business has suffered as a result." He turned and looked out the window to put an end to the conversation.

"Father, I cannot marry this boy, and I will not. I would rather learn a trade and work with my aunt in the cigar factory." Muriel spoke softly as she turned to leave the study. Her father still faced away from her. Glancing over her shoulder, she noticed that his back was hunched, as if a great weight held it down.

Straightening her shoulders, Muriel left to find her aunt. Although her aunt's husband's cigar factory was not a place for children she was determined to make her own way. She would be thirteen the following month when school let out for the summer. She would persuade her aunt to let her apprentice in the office and her uncle in each of the factory's stations during the summer. In the fall, she would learn all she could about other businesses and about the shipping trade from every relative who would teach her. With all her family's connections in the Keys, she could help her father's business. She could prove that she could become an independent woman and choose her husband.

New Providence, The Bahamas, was the largest island town in the Caribbean. The year was 1907 and the various islands were bustling with old and new businesses. It was settled by British immigrants who enjoyed the tropical breezes and building up their family's wealth. They created plantations, cornered local markets, financed new businesses, captained all the merchant and passenger ships, and stuck together. Most of the British sons and daughters were sent back to England to finish their education and to bring back suitable mates. If they could not find a suitable partner in England, they contracted with one the of other prominent British Bahamian families in marriage. They strived to keep their lineage pure and strong. The Roberts family of New Providence was such a family.

The Robertses' oldest son was prepared to inherit the family empire but their middle son, William Albert Roberts, had always dreamed of going to sea and making his place in the United States. The British inheritance law for prominent families did not suit him. William firmly believed that anyone who worked hard could accomplish great things. It should not matter where you were from or who your relatives were. His burning wish was to make his own way. to become a US citizen, and to own land somewhere near the Gulf of Mexico, the

WHERE TRADE WINDS MEET

Atlantic Ocean, or even the Pacific in the States. He also wanted a wife who would be a helpmate, not a society lady who only wanted to buy new clothes and attend prominent people's parties.

William had just turned sixteen this summer. He went to the docks and signed up with the first ship that would have him. He was not use to hard physical labor but he was determined to learn. Thus, he began his sea career as a deck hand.

Over the next few years, he traveled on various ships all around the Caribbean—picking up foodstuffs, tobacco leaves, cotton, sugar, and passengers and dropping them off at their various destinations—he learned each position on the crew. William crewed with three different boats and managed a few voyages up the Atlantic Coast to Newport, Boston, and even New York City. Those towns excited him. Toward the end of his training, he saw snow for the first time while crewing on the SS *Olivette*.

All the ships on which William worked were owned by a New York-based company. He had made sure the company had nothing to do with the British Bahamian family that he no longer wished to be a part of. His hard work and dedication were recognized and, in the beginning of 1912, William, now age twenty-one, was awarded the position of second in command of the SS *Mascotte*. He had petitioned the company to help him gain US citizenship and, before the *Mascotte* arrived in Key West, the captain had good news: The company would sponsor William's citizenship application once he had proven himself in his new role. William was determined to do an excellent job and, with all his savings residing in the First National Bank of Key West, he felt closer to this goal.

CHAPTER 1

William Albert Roberts could not contain his excitement as he descended the gangplank of the SS *Mascotte*. His well-worn, but well-kept and polished, seaman's boots touched the sunbaked wood of the pier. The port buzzed like a tropical beehive, the thrum of commerce and conversation mingling with the salty tang of the sea air. William's gray eyes, wide with the eagerness of a child at a fair, scanned the Key West landscape and absorbed every palm tree's silhouette against the clear blue sky. It felt good to be on land once more. And the news the captain had given him earlier had spread through his body like wildfire. The company had agreed to sponsor him for citizenship! His dreams were finally coming true.

"Welcome to paradise," he murmured to himself, a grin spreading across his face as he adjusted the cap on his light-brown hair. William had seen many a port in his time, but none quite so vibrant, none that seemed to pulse with the very rhythm of freedom like Key West. His good news may be coloring his perspective just a bit but he did not care.

He set off from the dock, weaving his way through the lively streets. Vendors hawked their wares with flirtatious banter. Rows of colorful clapboard houses greeted him with open verandas, and the whirring of bicycle wheels accompanied the clopping of horses drawing carriages. It was a symphony of the new world, a place where every brick whispered opportunities.

The melodic twang of a guitar drifted from an open window, mixing with the scent of frying fish and fresh fruit. William couldn't help but tap his foot to the music. His body responded to its invitation to celebrate life. He watched a group of children playing stickball in an alley, their laughter punctuating the air almost as sweetly as the calls of the gulls above.

"Quite the sight, is it not?" a passerby remarked, noting William's rapt attention.

"Indeed, it is," William responded, the warmth of camaraderie clear in his voice.

The stranger smiled and tipped his hat before moving on.

As William continued his exploratory stroll, his mind danced with the possibilities in this bustling port town,. His new commission as second in command afforded him more money and more days of leave. He would add the money to his growing bank account and explore the area for a place for his future home. Key West was one of the largest towns in Florida he might fulfill his dream here.

He made his way to Mallory Square, where the local fishermen boasted about their catches. Their nets, heavy with the silver bounty of the ocean, glistened under the afternoon sun. William watched, fascinated by the deft hands that sorted the day's haul.

"Best snapper in the Keys!" one called out, his voice carrying over the hubbub.

William shook his head at the vendor as he was after a different kind of meal.

WHERE TRADE WINDS MEET

William paused at the corner of Duval and Front. A newspaper under his arm was inked with the headlines of the day. He had purchased it not for the news, but for the classifieds that sprawled across the back pages. He scanned the columns, searching for any opportunity that might anchor him here. He was eager to see the ads for land available in the Keys, or perhaps even further up in Florida. The Miami area was growing, or perhaps he would go further north to Tampa.

With the company's promise of sponsorship, William was now eager to explore possibilities for a home. He knew his hard work would help him along the path to claiming a piece of the American dream—an oath of allegiance just waiting to be sworn and a place to build of his very own.

Within the walls of Santos's bustling Cuban cigar factory, Muriel Victorine Russell was fulfilling her obligations and working toward her own dream of independence. Her glance flitted over ledgers and order forms with precision and she dispatched instructions to the workers with practiced ease. The scent of tobacco leaves hung thick in the air, a constant reminder of the industry that fueled Key West's economy—and part of her family's livelihood.

"Double-check those counts, please," she said, her voice carrying over the hum of activity. "We cannot afford mistakes on an order this size."

"Of course, Miss Russell," came the swift reply, a chorus of affirmation from one of the workers.

LJ GREEN

Despite the ceaseless demands of her position, Muriel managed each task with an efficiency that belied her years. At eighteen, she was the factory's youngest-ever head shipping agent, yet she wielded her role with the confidence of a seasoned veteran. She moved among the rows of crates and bundles, ensuring that every cigar destined for distant shores left her charge in perfect condition.

She had achieved much by working side by side with her aunt and the others these last five years. There were fewer cigar factories in town now. Most of the others had moved up to Tampa after the great fire destroyed most of Key West in 1886. Hurricanes in 1909 and 1910 had damaged those that remained. Her family's factory had received only minor damage, and thanks to her aunt's negotiation skills, they had kept most of their suppliers in Cuba and their clients in the northern states. Sadly, that was her aunt's final accomplishment before turning over the reins to Muriel. Her aunt had developed a kidney disease and sought treatment from fancy doctors, the Mayo brothers, in Rochester, Minnesota.

As Muriel returned to her desk to review another stack of paperwork, the afternoon light streaming through the tall factory windows glinted off her hair, casting a warm glow around her. She allowed herself a small smile, proud her part in the continued prosperity of the Cuban side of her family. Some of the Conch side still worked in the factory too, but most pursued various other trades on their little island.

The sun dipped toward the horizon, painting the sky in hues of orange and pink and signaling the end of another productive day. Muriel swiped at her brows trying to relieve the tension from squinting at the numbers all day and closed the ledger with a soft thud. She stepped out into the balmy evening air, ready to board the electric trolley that would carry her homeward.

The next day found Muriel leaning against the door frame of the factory, her gaze traveling past the sun-soaked streets of Key West to the harbor where schooners and steamships whispered promises of distant lands. The salty breeze tugged at her light-brown hair and teased her with scents from faraway places. This week she had been wishing for a change in her life—like the hurricanes that blew away the old or tried to. She felt she had learned all that she could at the factory. She had saved a tidy sum and had trained her aunt's daughter, Cleora Fay Santos, in the various aspects of managing the business's shipping and inventory processes. Cleora had been eager to learn a trade and working for her relatives would give her a good start.

"Miss Russell, another order just came in," called out a worker, snapping Muriel back to reality.

"Thank you. I'll be right there," she replied, tucking a stray lock behind her ear. Within the walls of the factory, the air was thick with tobacco as she plodded through everyday tasks. But beyond these walls, her heart galloped toward the unknown, yearning for the day when she would cast off the shackles of her stale routine and visit far-off places with different climates.

William sauntered through the busy streets with the ease of a man unburdened by expectations. He continued to marvel at the kaleidoscope of colors adorning the marketplace, the vibrant fabrics fluttering like captured fragments of a rainbow. A group of children dashed past him, their laughter echoing through the square as they chased an errant ball. William couldn't help but smile; their joy was infectious, their freedom something he longed to capture for himself for today.

"Fresh conch! Get your fresh conch here!" a vendor shouted, adding his voice to the symphony of commerce and community that reverberated through Key West.

William paused, considering the delicacy, then shaking his head as he moved on. There were too many flavors to taste and too many sights to behold. He knew other places in the country were different, and he wanted to explore those as well. This minor part of America was familiar like home. He was ready for the next phase of his life. But for today, he would enjoy where he was.

Back at the Santos cigar factory, Muriel oversaw the loading of crates. Her movements were precise, her mind elsewhere. She imagined herself aboard a ship cutting through the cerulean waves, exploring ancient ruins and exotic markets—her life an endless expedition.

"Miss Russell, we're all set here," said a worker, jerking Muriel from her daydream once more.

"Excellent work," she praised, her voice carrying the weight of responsibility that never seemed to lighten.

WHERE TRADE WINDS MEET

Seated at her desk in the office, Muriel thumbed the edge of a crisp banknote, her weekly pay, tucking it into her bank book for later deposit. Around her, the hum of the factory was dulling to a whisper as another day's work drew to a close. She paused, leaning against the wooden counter that had borne witness to countless transactions under her watchful eye, and allowed herself a moment's indulgence.

"Paris ... Cairo ... the Far East ..." she whispered each destination like a sacred incantation, her eyes and face alight with possibility. Each name represented a siren's call to the soul of this island-bound dreamer. Her fingers traced the world map embossed on the cover of the savings book where her pay was recorded. With every penny scrimped from her salary, the weight of Key West's shores was reduced. The rising tide of her growing travel fund buoyed her spirit.

"Miss Russell, you're talking to your money again," chided Mr. Peters, the factory floor manager. His tone was teasing but not unkind.

"Because it's going to take me places," she retorted with a playful smile, then thumped the book with a satisfying slap. She rose and walked out the door, casting a smile to Mr. Peters as she left.

Stepping out into the early evening, Muriel made her way to the trolley stop, her thoughts adrift in visions of exotic lands. The trolley arrived with a friendly ding, the gas lights already lit and spilling their soft glow onto the road like liquid amber. She climbed aboard, taking her usual spot by the window.

She settled into her seat, her eyes reflecting the twilight sky outside. Yet, even as she rode through Key West, she was miles away, dancing across the globe in her reveries.

For Muriel, the trolley's path was all too familiar, etched into her daily existence like the grooves on a well-worn coin. But tonight, something felt different in the air, a shift so subtle it might have been missed had she not been so attuned to the whispers of change. She watched as a handsome young man quickened his pace to catch the trolley at the next stop.

William tipped his hat at a woman he passed when he heard the trolley coming up behind him. He quickened his pace to get to the next stop in time to board. When the car clanged to a stop he climbed in.

"Evening," he greeted the conductor, tipping his hat and paid his fee.

"Good evening, sir," replied the conductor with a nod and a smile.

The trolley car jostled forward, picking up speed along the tracks that ribboned through the heart of town. William moved toward the center of the car with the ease of a seasoned seaman to stand in the center holding onto the metal bar running the length of the car.

Muriel couldn't help but notice the newcomer. Perhaps it was the way he carried himself, or the faint scent of brine that clung to his clothes, telling tales of voyages she longed to embark upon. Their gazes met in a fleeting exchange, azure meeting slate gray. A silent acknowledgment spoke volumes in the briefest of moments. It was as if the universe itself conspired to draw two kindred spirits together—an adventurer filled with wanderlust and a woman whose dreams soared far beyond the horizon.

WHERE TRADE WINDS MEET

"Excuse me, miss," William said, breaking the spell as he reached past her to grasp the overhead strap. His voice carried the lilt of distant shores.

"Of course," Muriel replied. As she shifted to give him room, the corners of her mouth lifted in an involuntary smile.

The trolley bell clanged a sharp note that resonated with the pulse of Key West itself. William steadied himself as the car jerked forward again, his hand brushing Muriel's sleeve—a whisper of contact that sent ripples through the stillness between them. From their stolen glance, an unvoiced understanding unfurled, delicate as the lace trim on her blouse, resilient as the ship's rigging that had weathered tempests under his watch.

Muriel broke eye contact first and looked out the nearest window. Pastel-hued houses blurred into a watercolor streak of sun-washed walls and blooming bougainvillea in the twilight. Yet, her senses remained acutely aware of the man standing beside her.

"Beautiful evening, is it not?" William ventured, breaking the silent reverie that held her captive. His tone was light, but his eyes searched hers for some sign of kinship.

"It is," she replied, her voice tinged with the warmth of the setting sun. "The kind of day that makes you wish you could just sail away to anywhere."

"Anywhere but here?" He echoed her sentiment, a half-smile playing on his lips.

"Especially here," Muriel affirmed.

Their conversation danced around the edges of propriety: two strangers bound by the unspoken kinship of souls craving adventure. They spoke of the weather and of the places they passed along their short journey. Beneath the banter was recognition—an acknowledgment of the wanderlust that thrummed in their veins.

As the trolley neared its next stop, the spell of their encounter waned, giving way to the reality of their separate lives. William offered a polite nod, a gesture that belied the significance of their meeting. "Perhaps I'll see you around, miss."

"Perhaps," Muriel responded, the word lingering like the aftertaste of a bittersweet chocolate.

With a last glance that held the weight of uncharted futures, William stepped off the trolley and onto the crowded sidewalk, disappearing into the throng of townsfolk and tourists. Muriel watched his retreating form, her heart hitching at the thought of all that "perhaps" could mean in the future?

As the trolley moved on, the air still hummed with the electricity of their encounter. As Muriel's journey resumed, the anticipation of what might bloom from this chance meeting settled in her chest.

CHAPTER 2

The clinking of porcelain and the rich aroma of brewed coffee mingled with salty sea air at the bustling cafe where Muriel had met her confidantes. The establishment, nestled in the heart of Key West, thrummed with patrons' chatter and occasional laughter rising above the hum of conversation. As Muriel stepped inside, her gaze swept the room—short neatly brushed heads of the men and the crisp linen dresses worn by the women—before landing on two familiar faces.

"Over here, Muriel!" called Frieda Garfunkel, her voice a bright beacon amid the din. She waved exuberantly from their usual corner table. Mabel Knowles sat beside her, a mischievous twinkle in her eyes.

Muriel navigated the maze of tables with effortless grace, her light-brown hair catching the sunlight that filtered through the windows. Today a palpable excitement seemed to dance in her blue eyes.

Arriving at the table, Muriel apologized for being late, but her friends' warm smiles assured her that no offense was taken.

"Tell us everything," Mabel urged, leaning forward with eager anticipation. "Did you come up with any new plans for your great escape?" Her playful tone belied the genuine interest of her question; after all, it was not every day one heard of a woman dreaming of voyages beyond the safe harbor of Key West.

"Escape is right," Muriel laughed, settling into her chair. The server arrived with her order—a cup of strong Cuban coffee. Its steam curled skyward like the tendrils of far-off dreams. She wrapped her hands around the warm ceramic and gathered her thoughts.

"Imagine it, exploring foreign lands, tasting exotic foods, and walking streets that tell tales older than our own nation." Muriel's musing painted vivid pictures that pulled her friends into her aspirations. The gleam in her eyes intensified as she spoke of Parisian boulevards and Venetian canals and her lightly tanned complexion flushed with the thrill of endless possibilities.

"Every time you describe it, I feel like I'm already there," Frieda said, leaning back in her chair. Her expression was a mixture of longing and admiration. Her own future—dreary days attending the family's department store—loomed ahead, a stark contrast to Muriel's grand dreams.

"Ah, but we mustn't just dream. We have to act," Muriel declared. Her determination was clear in her posture, straight and unwavering like the mast of a ship set to sail. "I want to see it all, not from stories or postcards, but with my own eyes."

"Then you shall," Mabel affirmed, squeezing Muriel's arm in solidarity. "You've got more spirit than most men who captain those ships. If anyone can find a way, it's you, Muriel."

Their laughter blended once again with the ambient sounds of the cafe, a symphony of friendship and shared dreams that resonated within the walls of their beloved luncheon spot. As they sipped their coffee, the golden glow of the afternoon sun bathed the cafe in a warm light, sealing the moment—a snapshot of hope.

WHERE TRADE WINDS MEET

Muriel leaned forward, her hands sketching the arc of her envisioned travels in the air. The clink of porcelain and murmur of customers around them faded as Frieda's and Mabel's faces became mirrors of her excitement.

"Imagine stepping onto new lands, learning from each place I go!" Muriel's voice danced with her dreams.

Frieda's own longing for adventure was ignited by Muriel's passion. "Of course you must go, Muriel," Frieda exclaimed with youthful exuberance. "It's not every day that one of us gets to break free from these island shores."

"Absolutely," Mabel chimed in, her enthusiasm a beacon of encouragement.

Their coffee forgotten; the trio huddled closer as the world of the cafe shrank to just their table. Mabel tilted her head as an idea dawned.

"Wait—what about joining the Peninsular and Oriental Steam Navigation Company?" Mabel suggested, her voice a conspiratorial whisper. "You know P & O has been building more and more luxury passenger ships. And I've heard tales of stewardesses serving aboard—imagine the people you'd meet, the places you'd see!"

"Stewardess?" Muriel's brow lifted, considering a role not contemplated. "Serving the wealthy?" She mulled over the words. "I do not know if I could go from being in charge of shipping to serving the wealthy, cleaning up their messes, arranging their food, etcetera ..."

"I do know, Muriel," Mabel said. "You have the poise, the smarts, the patience ... and if it gets you to those exotic places you want to visit, why not?"

"Exploring new destinations while earning a living," Frieda mused, nodding in agreement. Her earlier discontent with her job was now overshadowed by the thrill of Muriel's prospective journey.

"Could it really be possible?" Muriel pondered aloud, her gaze through the window. The ambitious idea settled into her thoughts like an anchor finding its hold on the vast ocean floor.

"Let's find out," Mabel said, her smile as promising as the horizon. "But first, another round of coffee. We've got grand plans to brew."

Muriel swirled the last of her coffee in the cup, the dark liquid chasing its own tail. "But what if there's more? What if I could do something ... unique?"

"Unique?" Frieda leaned in, mischief dancing in her hazel eyes. "You mean more than just serving tea and scones to high society on the high seas?"

"Exactly." Muriel set down her cup and lowered her voice as if divulging a secret. "I can navigate conversations in Spanish, Italian, some Greek, and French. That has to be worth something on those international voyages."

"Of course!" Frieda snapped her fingers as the idea materialized before them. "You could work as a translator or interpreter! Imagine the doors it would open, not just for you, but for all the passengers needing guidance across language barriers."

"True," Muriel said, her mind alight with visions of herself, bridging worlds with nothing but her words. She had honed these skills through years of haggling and bantering at the cigar factory.

WHERE TRADE WINDS MEET

"Though," Mabel interjected, pouring a touch of reality into their dream-soaked conversation, "it will not be easy. As women ... well, we're expected to keep to certain roles, aren't we?"

"Seeing a woman assert herself in such a position will raise eyebrows, maybe even cause a stir," Frieda added, her tone somber yet defiant.

"Then let them stare," Muriel said, her posture stiffening and her eyes brimmed with determination. "I'll show them that my mind is every bit as capable as any man's. Besides, it's about time those societal expectations met with a minor challenge. Do you agree?"

Mabel nodded, her smile returning. "You'll need an introduction, perhaps from one of your affluent clients at the factory. And a couple of reference letters wouldn't hurt."

"Agreed. It's a good thing I've kept up friendly relations with Mr. Antonio Carrasco of the Cuban Consulate and Dr. Myrtle M. Seiler. They travel quite a bit so their references might carry weight." Muriel's practicality shone through as resolve flushed her cheeks.

"Resilience and determination," Frieda said, lifting her cup in a toast. "That's how we'll arm ourselves."

"Alongside our wit and charm," Mabel added with a wink, clinking her cup against theirs.

Their laughter echoed once again. The harmonious sound belied the steel they'd need to forge their paths in a world not quite ready for women to defy the tide.

"Every step of the way, Muriel," Frieda affirmed, reaching across the table to squeeze her friend's hand. Her own eyes were alight with shared fervor. "You will not be boarding that ship alone—not really. Our spirits will be right there with you."

"Consider us your anchor and your sails," Mabel chimed in,. "We'll be here to keep you grounded or to push you forward whenever you need it."

"Thank you," Muriel replied, her heart swelling with gratitude. The camaraderie of her friends was a lifeline, a navigational chart for the journey she was plotting.

The soft clink of cutlery and gentle murmur of conversation provided a melodic backdrop as the three young women leaned into their shared resolve.

"Let's make a pact," Muriel suggested. Her gaze flitted from Frieda to Mabel, locking onto an unspoken understanding that had always tethered their trio.

"Here and now," Frieda agreed, her chin raised in silent challenge to any who'd dare question their mettle.

"To support each other's dreams," Mabel continued, the corners of her mouth curving upward with determination. "To seize every chance that comes our way, no matter how daunting."

"Without fear," Muriel concluded, the lowering sun igniting a fire behind her. "For we are more than the roles society has cast for us. We are adventurers, charting our own course."

Their hands came together in the center of the table, fingers entwining in a symbol of unity that felt as ancient as the sea itself. In that singular moment, as midday gave way to late afternoon, and the warm glow of the cafe sheltered them from the encroaching dusk, they were no longer Muriel, Frieda, and Mabel. They were a fellowship set upon changing tides.

WHERE TRADE WINDS MEET

As Muriel smiled at her two friends, a picture of the handsome young man on the trolley invaded her mind. A tiny voice said, "There might be a third choice."

CHAPTER 3

As William strolled down Duval Street, he cut a dashing figure among the crowd in his pressed, sharply creased uniform and shining insignia. His light-brown hair caught the glimmer of the morning sun as he dodged vendors hawking their wares and fishermen boasting of their catches. The scent of salt and citrus hung in the air, mingling with the less savory odors of fish and sweat. Each step on the bricks seemed to echo his determination for a future with lands of his own in the Americas and perhaps a worthy companion at his side. He thought of the pretty young woman on the trolley the previous day. There was a spark there. He only had a few more days of shore leave left before moving on to the next port of call. Perhaps he would see her again. That thought had him smiling brighter still.

"Excuse me, sir! Fresh oranges, sweet as sunshine!" called out a fruit seller, but William only smiled and continued on his way.

Meanwhile, at the factory, Muriel stood amid rows of workers. A few tendrils of her light-brown hair escaped a practical bun to frame her slightly tanned complexion as her hands deftly sorted through the completed cigars prior to packing. Her blue eyes, reflecting the clear Floridian skies, now held a distant gleam, as if she envisioned herself in far-off lands. Shaking her head at her wayward thoughts she couldn't recall the last few items she handled. Distraction overwhelmed her.

"Miss Russell, this case needs your approval for shipping," a worker said, snapping Muriel back to reality.

"Of course. Just a moment," she replied, her warm voice tinged with an undercurrent of restlessness. It was not the shipping labels that intrigued her most, but the many destinations they bore—Atlanta, Washington, D.C., Boston, New York, and even Spain, England, and Greece. Recalling that Cleora was waiting for her for the next lesson on business ledgers and procedures, she shook her head again in derision. "I have to get back to work and stop this daydreaming," she mumbled.

Later that afternoon, William stepped aboard the electric trolley, its cables humming with energy. Excitement was palpable in his quickened pulse. He found himself surrounded by a mosaic of passengers: businessmen perusing newspapers, mothers corralling children, and young couples stealing furtive glances.

Just as the trolley was about to lurched forward, Muriel slipped through its doors, her gaze scanning for an empty seat. Her presence drew the attention of those around her; her stature and confident air set her apart from the other commuters. She clutched a small leather satchel containing her meticulously drawn maps and charts of parts of the world she longed to see. These were secret treasures that she was taking away from the prying eyes of the factory and her new student, Cleora.

WHERE TRADE WINDS MEET

As the trolley trundled along Whitehead Street, the two dreamers sat opposite each other, unaware of the shared passions simmering beneath their composed exteriors. William adjusted his cap, his fingers brushing the emblem of his station. Muriel turned her face toward the window, where the tropical landscape blurred into a watercolor of greens and blues.

William's gaze drifted over the assembly of faces. As the vehicle rocked a slow back and forth cadence on its tracks, it was as if fate nudged his attention across the aisle. His eyes met Muriel's. In that suspended moment, an unspoken understanding passed between them—a mutual recognition of souls yearning for the world beyond these shores.

"Excuse me," William ventured, his voice tinged with an accent born of sun-kissed Bahamian breezes. "I couldn't help noticing your satchel. A fellow traveler, perhaps?"

Muriel's lips curved into a soft smile, her blue eyes brightening. "In dreams, certainly. And you? Do your journeys extend past these waters?" Her voice was a subtle mixture of her Cuban family and the more local Key West Conch.

"Indeed, they do," he replied. The seat next to her became available and he moved to sit beside her, the trolley resuming its gentle swaying. "I'm the second officer on the *Mascotte*. She's a fine ship, takes me to Tampa, here, and Havana, and back again. But it's the 'back again' that weighs heavy."

"Because the heart wants what lies at the end of the next horizon?" Muriel asked, her voice a melodious blend of curiosity and understanding.

"Exactly," William affirmed, nodding. "I want to see the pyramids of Egypt, the markets of Bombay, to witness the endless variety of this grand world."

"Ah, to walk through the ruins of ancient Rome," Muriel mused, her eyes alight with shared fervor. "To traverse the Great Wall of China, to sail around Cape Horn." Her enthusiasm seemed to fill the surrounding space, drawing William in further.

"Those are bold aspirations for a woman of Key West," William observed, admiration lacing his words.

"Perhaps," Muriel conceded with a tilt of her head, "but why should my dreams be any less vast than yours? Just because my days are spent in the confines of a factory doesn't mean my thoughts must remain there."

"Of course not," William agreed, his heart quickening at the depth behind her gaze. "We're all bound by the same stars, aren't we? No matter where we're anchored."

Their conversation flowed like the currents of the sea—effortless, exploratory, each revelation of their inner landscapes forging a connection as potent as the tropical air enveloping the island. The streets of Key West rolled by outside the trolley windows, but inside, William and Muriel traversed distances far greater than mere geography could define.

As the trolley clattered along the iron rails, William, with a gaze cast out to the vibrant streets of Key West, shifted in his seat. His elbow brushed against something soft—a hand, Muriel's hand. He turned, half-apologetic, only to catch the tail end of a smile dancing on her lips before she looked away. The touch was fleeting, but it sent a charge through them that lingered like the warm afterglow of a setting sun.

"I beg your pardon," he murmured, though his feelings about the accidental encounter were anything but regretful.

WHERE TRADE WINDS MEET

"No need," Muriel replied, her voice low and tinged with amusement. "One could say it's just the trolley bringing people together."

William chuckled, noting the crinkles around her eyes when she smiled. He stole quick glances at her. Each look they shared was a silent acknowledgment, an affirmation of the unexpected connection forming between them.

"Please forgive me." William tilted his head with a slight bow. "My name is William Albert Roberts." His eyes twinkled with challenge.

Muriel extended her hand, "And I am Muriel Victorine Russell." Her whole body seemed to shine with delight as their hands met in a brief shake. They both lapsed into silence for a moment.

"Tell me, Miss Russell," William started.

"Please call me Muriel."

Nodding in acknowledgment, he continued, "What is it you fear the most in chasing these dreams of yours?"

Muriel pondered the question, glancing toward the window where palm trees swayed in rhythm with the ocean breeze. "I suppose ... I fear I might wake up one day, old and gray, realizing that life has passed me by without my ever having truly lived it, without ever seeing the world beyond this island."

"Ah, the curse of unspent time," William said, nodding thoughtfully. "I share that fear. Out there, on the open sea, I feel alive. But once we dock, the weight of expectation settles in, and I wonder if I'll ever break free from the anchor of routine."

"Routine can be comforting, though," Muriel countered, turning to him with a gentle tilt of her head. "But it's the possibility of what lies beyond the horizon that makes the heart race, is it not?"

Their conversation ebbed and flowed. A dynamic tide of hopes and aspirations surged between them. They spoke of the stars that guided sailors and dreamers alike, of the injustice of dreams deferred, and of the relationships that anchored them yet also set them adrift.

The trolley clattered along the tracks, its electric hum a steady undercurrent to the murmur of voices within. William leaned back against the wooden bench and let his gaze drift toward Muriel. Her profile showed concentration as she considered their previous exchange. He admired the way her brow knitted in thought. Then she turned to face him, the tropical light streaming into the windows casting a soft glow on her skin.

"William, my family ..." Muriel began, her voice trailing off as she searched for the right words. "They see a certain path for me—marriage, children, a life rooted here in Key West."

"Rooted," he echoed, understanding the weight of the word. "My own family, they couldn't fathom why I'd wanted to go to sea. To them, it's as if I've chosen to cast away our traditions, to set sail on a fool's errand."

"Yet, here you are," Muriel said, a wry smile playing on her lips. "A second officer, no less. You must have quite the rebellious streak."

"Perhaps," William conceded with a chuckle. "Or maybe it's just the call of the sea; it can be louder than any disapproving voice."

Their laughter mingled, and for a moment, the social expectations that bound them seemed to dissolve into the warm air of the trolley car. The vehicle continued its journey, the gentle sway lulling the passengers into a shared rhythm as if the very heart of Key West beat through the soles of their shoes.

"Time has a peculiar way of slipping by when one is ... engrossed," William remarked, his eyes not leaving hers.

"Engrossed?" Muriel repeated the corner of her mouth quirked up in amusement.

"Certainly," he replied, leaning closer, his voice dropping to a conspiratorial whisper. "When two kindred spirits share a vision of the world beyond, time becomes nothing more than an afterthought."

"Kindred spirits," Muriel mused. "I like the sound of that. But time, Mr. Roberts, is something we cannot escape, even if we wish to."

"True," he said, nodding. "And yet, I cannot but wonder if time is not also our ally, giving us the chance to ... to navigate these waters together."

"Navigate, explore, discover," Muriel added, each word punctuated with a hopeful undertone. "One could almost forget the shore when the current feels this inviting."

"Almost," William agreed, the hint of a promise in his tone.

"Miss Russell," William said, his voice resonant with newfound resolve. "Might I be so bold as to say that this conversation has been the most extraordinary voyage I've embarked upon in quite some time?"

"Mr. Roberts," Muriel responded, her eyes shining with equal parts daring and delight. "I believe we have only just hoisted the sails."

Outside the trolley car windows, the world of Key West unfurled like a painting brought to life. Palm trees lined the sidewalks, their fronds dancing in the salty breeze with a grace that echoed the swaying skirts of passing women. The sun dipped lower in the sky, bathing the streets below in a golden hue that seemed to ignite the very air with an amber glow. From somewhere beyond the clapboard houses and cigar shops, the murmur of the ocean whispered promises of distant shores along with a lone whistle of the train so recently delivered to the area.

William glanced out the window, his gray eyes reflecting the vivid scenery. He had seen many a sunset on the open sea, but there was something about this one, shared in Muriel's company, that felt different. It was as if the setting sun was not signaling the day's end, but the beginning of something new and thrilling.

"Key West does put on quite the show, doesn't it?" Muriel mused, her gaze following his.

"It certainly does," William agreed, turning back to her with a smile. "Nature's palette seems generous here."

The trolley bell clanged, heralding their approach to the next stop. A flutter of anticipation stirred in William's chest, not for the destination, but for the promise of future encounters. He reached into his black naval officer's coat, drawing forth a small, creased notebook and a stub of pencil. Scribbling, he tore out the page and handed it to Muriel.

"Here, Miss Russell, my contact at the docks. I ... We should continue this exploration of ideas, perhaps over a walk by the harbor?"

Muriel's fingers brushed against his as she accepted the slip of paper, sending a thrill through him that rivaled the electric charge powering their transport. Her blue eyes sparkled with a playful light as she rummaged through her purse, producing a small card, which she handed to him

"Mr. Roberts, you'll find me most agreeable to the idea," she said, the corner of her mouth lifting in a coy smile.

Their hands lingered for a moment longer than necessary, both reluctant to sever the connection. As the trolley slowed to a halt, passengers rose from their seats, a symphony of shuffling feet and murmured farewells filling the surrounding space.

"Until then," William said, standing to let her pass, his voice tinged with a hope that felt as vast as the ocean itself.

"Until then," Muriel echoed. Before descending the steps, she paused with a backward glance that spoke volumes.

As the trolley resumed its journey, the palm fronds continued to sway, and the distant sound of waves caressed the island's edges. In those last moments before the trolley carried William away from Muriel, the air seemed charged with the promise of adventures yet to come, of uncharted territories in both the world and the heart.

The trolley rattled onward, leaving a trail of electric hum in its wake. William craned his neck to catch one last glimpse of her retreating figure, the hem of her skirt fluttering like a pennant in the sea breeze as she walked down a side street. Despite the trolley's clamor and the chatter of its remaining passengers, William's world had narrowed to the memory of Muriel's smile, the warmth of her hand, and the anticipation of seeing her again.

"Quite the day, ain't it?" the trolley's driver called back over his shoulder, a knowing grin spreading across his weathered face. William could only nod, his mind adrift on the swell of new emotions.

"Indeed," he replied. His voice, just above a whisper, was lost amid the gentle clink of the trolley's workings and the rustling of palmettos in the salty air.

As the trolley approached his stop, William rose, his movements automatic but his thoughts still anchored to Muriel. As he approached the exit, the weight of his seaman's uniform served as a stark reminder of the life he led—yet his thoughts were consumed by the life he yearned for, one filled with shared adventures and whispered dreams beneath foreign stars.

Disembarking with a polite nod to the driver, William stepped onto the brick street that led to the harbor. The scent of brine and fish filled his nostrils, mingling with the faint, lingering fragrance of Muriel's perfume that seemed to cling to his senses. He walked with the purpose of a man on a mission, not just of duty but of desire.

"An officer and a gentleman," he muttered to himself, "and now a suitor." The words felt strange, yet thrilling like the first daring leap into uncharted waters.

Behind him, the trolley bell clanged its departure, leaving behind the echo of laughter and conversation. But within William, a silent vow was forming a promise to cast aside the constraints of his social standing and pursue the woman who had, in a single trolley ride, captivated his heart.

CHAPTER 4

The sun had barely crested the horizon, painting the early morning sky in soft hues of pink and orange as William Roberts leaned on the rail and took in a deep calming breath. Anticipation raced through him. A stark contrast to the calm seas he gazed upon from the deck of the SS *Mascotte*. However, today he had to put the sea on hold. He had been so excited when he received Muriel's note asking him to call her at the factory that morning. He did not know where the nearest telephone box was but was told by several people he passed along his way that the Key West bank had one he could use. Why he did not just go to her office he could not say. When he was connected to her office, they agreed to meet the next morning at the trolley stop near her house.

Outside the bank, William jumped with joy, then almost floated back to the ship. He had much to do to get ready for this momentous meeting with Muriel. He hustled by the outdoor vendors without even acknowledging their calls. Breaking stride, he remembered he needed to eat. He grabbed bread from one vendor, then cooked chicken with rice from another. Near the ship he found some oranges and bananas for dessert.

Once he was aboard, he confirmed with his captain what he needed to accomplish to have a whole day to himself. When he received his captain's confirmation, he bounced out of the room, still a bundle of energy and smiles, to complete his task list. He wanted to finish all his chores and make sure he had clean civilian clothes to wear.

After wishing the lad well, the crusty captain smiled as he returned to his charts and the log. The eager young officer's look of anticipation must have indicated he had met a young lass. Shaking his head, the captain grumbled about the delays in repairs his ship needed.

***

William spotted Muriel from a distance. Her light-brown hair, worn in a more casual style, caught the early morning rays of sunlight. Her skin seemed to glow with the same excitement that bubbled within him. As their eyes met, a silent acknowledgment passed between them—a shared thrill for the day's impending adventures.

"Good morning, Muriel," William greeted. "I trust you slept well?" He held out his hand to help Muriel up into the trolley.

"Better than I have in weeks, knowing today I would spend with you," she replied, her sparkling eyes dancing. "And you, William? Ready to trade the ship's deck for the streets of my hometown?"

"More ready than you know," he admitted with a smile. They moved down the aisle to seats near the middle of the car.

As the trolley hummed into motion, William turned to face Muriel. "What marvels does Key West hold for us today?"

Muriel's eyes lit up as she spoke, her passion for her home clear in every word. "We shall start at the lighthouse. I have obtained permission from the keeper, Mrs. Bethel, for us to

WHERE TRADE WINDS MEET

visit. It is quite a climb, but the view from the top is worth every step. You can see the entire island, and on a clear day like this, the water is an endless canvas of blues and greens."

"Sounds perfect," William murmured, his mind already imagining the sight. The trolley rumbled beneath them, a soothing vibration that complemented the flow of their conversation.

"Then perhaps a stroll along the beach of your Atlantic Ocean? It's not as dramatic a view as the one back home, but it has a charm all its own, I hear," he suggested, his tone teasing.

"William," Muriel laughed, the sound blending with the clack of the trolley tracks, "you are about to learn that everything in Key West has its own unique charm."

"Is that so?" he said, arching an eyebrow. "Well then, I am in the hands of the best guide Key West offers."

"Indeed, you are. But let us not forget—we have the entire island to explore after the lighthouse."

Their plans unfurled like the sails of a ship catching a favorable wind. Each idea built upon the last, revealing the depth of their curiosity and the strength of their burgeoning bond. William listened, his admiration for Muriel's knowledge and love for her city growing with every descriptive detail she wove into their itinerary.

"Today feels like the beginning of something remarkable," Muriel mused, her gaze meeting William's.

"Yes, it does," he agreed.

The rattle and hum of the trolley car's mechanisms serenaded William and Muriel as they leaned into each other, sharing a warmth that was only partially due to the early Florida sun. Outside, Key West stretched and yawned into life.

William watched as pastel-hued homes with gingerbread trim flickered by, their vibrant shades a stark contrast to the staid colors of the Nassau architecture he knew so well.

"Look there," Muriel pointed. Her arm brushed against his as she gestured toward a group of children dashing across the street. Their laughter rose above the noise of the trolley. "The spirit of the island is in its youth—ever playful, always daring."

William smiled, appreciating Muriel's affection for her hometown. "Key West truly is full of life," he observed and noted the way her lips curved upward at his words. The trolley bell clanged as they neared their destination and their anticipation crackled like static in the sea air.

When the trolley lurched to a halt, Muriel and William stepped down onto the hard-packed shell street. They had left the cacophony of market bartering for the quieter, more historic part of town. Soon the Key West lighthouse loomed before them, its white façade a beacon of maritime history standing proudly against the azure sky.

"Shall we?" William asked, offering his hand with a gentlemanly flourish.

As their hands touched, a jolt of connection surged through them, unnoticed by the world but felt within.

"Yes," Muriel replied, her voice tinged with the thrill of shared adventure.

They approached the lighthouse keeper's house. Nodding her head to William she went through the gate and up the porch steps. Muriel's knock on the outer door was followed by a woman's loud reply. "Just a minute! I am coming."

William lifted an eyebrow as he recognized the accent of his homeland in the lady's voice. His posture stiffened with worry that he was about to be presented to someone who knew of his family.

Muriel looked at William questioningly but, before she could ask, Mrs. Bethel opened the door, smiling. "Welcome, child." She smiled at William as well. "Please go on back to the kitchen. We will have a spot of tea before you trek up those steps."

Muriel, who had visited the keeper before, took the lead. It was only polite to have a sit-down and a cup of tea with the lady. Her job was a lonely one and lonelier still since her husband, the assigned keeper, had passed the previous year. The lighthouse committee had not wanted to displace the widow, as she could continue the duties Mr. Bethel had shown her how to do.

"Mrs. Bethel, I would like to introduce my new friend, William Albert Roberts, of the SS *Mascotte*."

William continued to stand at attention, waiting for the woman to recognize his family name and perhaps blurt out his families' high-born prejudices to Muriel.

However, Mrs. Bethel just said, "Welcome to my home, Mr. Roberts," and indicated a seat.

William replied, "Thank you, Mrs. Bethel. It is a pleasure."

"Ah, I recognized that lilt in your voice. You from the Bahamas?"

"Yes, ma'am, I am."

"Lots of Robertses all around them islands. I miss it sometimes, but here in Key West it is pretty nice too." She smiled again as she poured out tea into each cup.

William relaxed completely when the lady did not seem to know who he or his family were. She just associated him with the mix of Robertses within the region and not with his specific family. Smiling in relief, he took a healthy swig of the cooling tea and reached for one of the cookies arranged on the plate in the center of the table.

After observing pleasantries and exchanging some gossip, Mrs. Bethel led them out to the back porch. She waved them on, saying, "You two be careful going up those metal steps and take your time."

Muriel led the way into the cool dimness of the lighthouse interior. The sudden change from sunlight to shadow caused her to stumble and William to quickly grasp her arm to steady her back on the walk. She smiled her thanks as they began to ascend the tower single file. The spiral staircase wound upward like the shell of a conch, beckoning them to uncover the secrets held aloft.

With their ascent, each, in turn, emitted a puff of laughter at the effort it took to gain altitude as the winding steps ascended the cement cylinder. Those sounds echoed off the walls. William marveled at how effortlessly Muriel moved, her familiarity with the lighthouse evident in the confident tilt of her head as she looked back at him over her shoulder.

"Almost there," Muriel encouraged. Her hand squeezed his as they neared the last steps, a symbolic gesture that spoke of support and unity even in the face of the unknown.

Upward they climbed, the rhythm of their ascent punctuated by the soft scuff of shoes on painted metal. As they reached the upper levels, the closeness of the stairwell gave way to a sense of vastness, an opening up of possibilities that mirrored the expanding horizon of their relationship.

WHERE TRADE WINDS MEET

Reaching the top, they paused, catching their breath not just from the exertion but also from the anticipation of what lay beyond the lighthouse door.

William pushed open the newly painted door and they stepped out onto the catwalk around the giant light. The morning light was bright and clear all around Key West. The city was a jewel floating on the sparkling turquoise sea. He watched Muriel's eyes widen with delight and reflect the vast expanse of water stretching to the horizon.

"It is magnificent," she breathed. Her voice was barely louder than the whispering wind that danced around them.

"More than words can say," William agreed. He stood close, sharing in the moment's reverence as they took in the panoramic views—the playful dance of palm fronds in the morning breeze, the distant sails of fishing boats, and the quaint houses dotting the shoreline like pastel-colored confections.

As they circled the gallery, their shoulders brushed in electric awareness. Muriel's eyes sparkled with joy, and William knew this was the perfect moment to peel back another layer of their aspirations.

"Tell me, Muriel," William began when they reached the entrance to the stairway once more, "what visions do you harbor for your future?"

She glanced at him, her gaze as earnest as her thoughts. "I dream of traveling," Muriel confessed. "To see Paris, London, the pyramids of Egypt. There is so much more beyond our little island." She looked into Williams earnest face and smiled while the soft breeze at the top of the tower lightly rustled her loosened hair.

"Traveling, yes, you mentioned that before," William mused, his own yearning stirring within him. "It's a fine dream, full of adventure and discovery."

"And you, William? What do you aspire to in this grand life?"

He took a breath, feeling the weight of his goal—and its importance. "To become a US citizen," he admitted in a whisper. "To truly belong in America, to make my mark here. Perhaps even ..." His voice trailed off, hesitant to reveal too much.

"Perhaps even what?" Muriel encouraged.

"To find a place to call home," he finished, his eyes locked with hers. "To have my own land and grow a family there."

Muriel's smile was soft as understanding flickered across her sun-kissed complexion. "A noble dream, William. One I hope you will achieve."

"Would you also consider putting down roots somewhere other than Key West, Muriel?"

"Yes, I believe I would. And William, would you be willing to continue traveling between planting roots and making a family?" She looked up at him, her face earnest as she waited for an honest reply.

"For you, I would and could do both things."

William gathered Muriel in his arms and he brushed a light kiss on her lips. His kiss contained all the longing and fervor built up over the last forty-eight hours and over the years of hoping to find a like-minded partner.

Muriel enjoyed the sensation of his lips on hers. Electricity radiated up and down her being. She stepped back, almost stumbling into the doorway to the stairs, but William cradled her until she regained her balance. She moved out of his arms, still holding his hand and looked down the stairs, "Let's get down to the bottom before we fall off." She laughingly replied.

Upon reaching the bottom safely they both stepped out and looked back up at the lighthouse. It was a beacon for travelers at sea but had now become a beacon for their dreams—a testament to the path they might forge together.

Muriel and William found a secluded spot on the Atlantic Beach side of the island, away from the few somewhat early risers wandering near the water's edge. They settled onto the cool sand, their shoes discarded, toes relishing the softness beneath them.

"William," Muriel began, her voice rising above the sound of the gentle waves. "There is something I must confess." Her gaze wavered, fixed on the shoreline where the sea caressed the land in a rhythmic dance, She released a pent-up sigh.

He turned toward her. The furrow of concern on her brow seemed out of place on such a serene morning. "What is it, Muriel?" His tone was steady, an anchor in the fluid uncertainty that surrounded them.

"My family ... they will not approve of us." The words spilled out. She looked at him then, her blue eyes searching for understanding. "They would see you as an outsider, someone who does not belong in our world."

William took a moment to absorb her words. He had not considered her family's disapproval, as people in New Providence considered him quite a catch. He was from the best of families in the Bahamas but hearing her say that he would not be a suitable mate for her sent him spiraling in another direction. Yet, he felt no anger, only a resolve that stemmed from something deeper than defiance.

"Your family's opinion, while important, does not define what we are to each other." His reply carried a calm certainty. "I too come from a prominent family in the Bahamas but their traditions and expectations should not define us now at the beginning of the twentieth century."

Muriel's lips curved into a fragile smile, bolstered by his reassurance. "But the obstacles, William. They are real and many."

"Obstacles can be navigated," he replied. "Just as a ship finds its way through treacherous seas, we too shall find our passage."

"Let us be like the sea, adaptable, enduring, and always finding our way home," she whispered.

Home. The word hung between them, ladened with meaning and the sweet anticipation of a future crafted by their own hands. On this quiet stretch of beach in Key West, as they held hands, they knew they would endure—as long as they faced all obstacles together.

They spent the rest of the day walking the streets, enjoying a snack and then a meal together, laughing, and enjoying each other's company. As they met different people along the way, Muriel spoke to each in their own language, shifting easily back to English to include William in the conversation.

Hand in hand, William and Muriel meandered through the streets of the city, their footfalls in sync with the gentle rhythm of island life. The sun, now low on the horizon, painted the sky with streaks of orange and purple. Its warm glow reflected off shop windows and cast long shadows. Laughter spilled from nearby taverns, merging with the strumming of a guitar and the soft clinking of glasses raised in toasts to the end of another day.

Their conversation flowed, sprinkled with anecdotes and shared dreams. Each revelation drew them closer in their forbidden dance. As they passed, they noticed Frieda's father's department store that proudly displayed the latest hats and dresses. They also caught the rich aroma of spiced conch chowder emanating from Mabel's restaurant.

"Imagine us traveling to all the places we have read about," Muriel said wistfully, gazing out to the different ships' masts and steam pipes rising high into the air along the harbor's boardwalk. "Paris, London ... even Egypt."

"Combining your knack for languages with my knowledge of the sea, we'll make it to every single one." William straightened his shoulders with pride that he was with someone so loved by her community, so smart and ambitious. His dreams of citizenship in the United States and of a settled life expanded to include grand adventures with Muriel.

"Yes, I have picked up quite a few languages over the years." Muriel smiled at the thought of learning even more.

As they made their way to her home, the afterglow of the setting sun still warmed their backs while the world around them quieted to a whisper. Their minds replayed the laughter shared atop the lighthouse, the awe of the panoramic views, the sweet passion of their first kiss, and the earnest confessions exchanged on the soft sands of the beach. Each recollection was a testament to their growing bond, a bond not even the staunchest disapproval could break.

"Home" was a concept both tangible and elusive, but as they reached the doorstep of Muriel's family's house, they understood that home was not a place. It was wherever they stood together, defiant in the face of convention, unwavering in their commitment to each other.

"Goodnight, Muriel," William said, his voice just above a whisper as he released her hand with reluctance.

"Goodnight, William," she replied, her smile lingering like the last rays of the sunset. "Thank you for today."

With a last glance over her shoulder, Muriel slipped indoors, her heart full and her spirit daring to believe that, come what may, their dreams were indeed within reach.

CHAPTER 5

In the shipping office of the Santos cigar factory, Muriel perched on the edge of her chair, her fingers absentmindedly tracing the grain of the wooden desk. The ledger before her held the day's accounts, but the numbers blurred into insignificance against the backdrop of her inner turmoil. In her mind, the memory of William's gray eyes seemed to cast a storm over the clear Key West sky. She found herself in a tempest of forbidden thoughts.

"Good heavens, Muriel, you look as if you're trying to solve the world's mysteries," came the teasing lilt of Frieda's voice as she breezed into the room. Muriel's gaze snapped from the window to the doorway. Frieda stood there, hands on hips, her youthful exuberance making light of the solemn mood.

Behind her, Mabel appeared, her smile as bright as the tropical sun. "Oh, let her be—perhaps she is," Mabel chimed in, her eyes crinkling in amusement.

The two friends flanked their confidante, their presence a gentle reminder of kindred spirits in a world bound by strict mores and expectations. They settled themselves across from Muriel, their skirts whispering against the floorboards, creating a feminine barrier of companionship between the outside world and the troubled young woman.

"Out with it then," Frieda urged. The concern in her dark eyes betrayed the levity in her voice. "You have been mooning about like one of those tragic heroines in the novels we adore."

"Indeed," Mabel agreed, reaching out to pat Muriel's hand. "This is not like you. You are the most level-headed one among us."

Muriel offered them a small, grateful smile. It was true—Frieda might dream of escaping her father's department store for a summer of flirtations, and Mabel's charm could enchant any diner into a better tip at the restaurant. But it was Muriel who they turned to when life became too tangled. Now it was she who needed untangling.

"Sometimes," Muriel began, her voice just above a whisper, "the heart does not so easily yield to the head." She left the thought hanging among them, knowing that her friends were astute enough to read between the lines.

"Ah," Frieda said, nodding sagely. "It is matters of the heart then."

"Yes, we saw you and that young sailor from the *Mascotte* eating at our restaurant Saturday," Mabel said, frowning just a little, "Mother would not let me come out and tease you."

"Girls," Muriel sighed, feeling the weight of confession on her lips, even as she held back the details. These two knew her well—too well. But even with the comfort of their solidarity, societal chains clanked on her conscience.

"Whatever it is," Frieda declared, her tone shifting to one of resolve, "we stand with you, Muriel—against fathers, against gossip, against this tiny island's idea of propriety."

"Indeed," echoed Mabel, her hand still on Muriel's. "We're your lifeboat, dear. No matter the storm."

Their words, simple and sincere, carved a space for courage in Muriel's conflicted heart. She looked at each friend, her allies in a battle she was only just beginning to fight, and felt the

WHERE TRADE WINDS MEET

inner stirring of the steely resolve of women who had come before. She wouldn't let the era's gender roles or the town's narrow view of propriety dictate her path.

"Thank you," Muriel whispered, buoyed by their unwavering support. "For listening, for understanding ..."

"Always," Frieda and Mabel said in unison.

With the ledger forgotten, the three sat in quiet solidarity, their bond a living testament to the strength found in shared struggles and enduring friendships.

Muriel's fingers trembled as they traced the edge of an envelope, the paper crisp and unmarred on her desk. Frieda leaned in, her curiosity a bright spark in her youthful eyes. "What's that? A letter to be sent out?"

"More like one that I wish I could write," Muriel confessed, the truth spilling from her in a rush of nervous energy.

"Go on," Mabel encouraged, her gaze soft and inviting.

"His name is William Roberts," Muriel began, her voice a hushed torrent of emotion. "I find myself thinking of him all the time. His smile, his voice ... it's as if he's anchored himself to my very soul."

Frieda's face lit up with a knowing grin, while Mabel's expression softened with empathy. "Oh, Muriel, that's wonderful! And terribly romantic," Frieda exclaimed, clasping her hands together.

"But it's not proper," Muriel fretted, wringing her hands. "He's a foreign officer, and I'm just ... a Conch."

"Proper be damned!" Frieda declared with a defiant toss of her light-brown hair. "Muriel, life is too short to let society dictate who we can love. Follow your heart and fight for what makes you happy. Besides, he's an officer and officers' wives can travel with them on civilian ships, especially those luxury liners we have been reading about."

"Your William sounds a fine gentleman," Mabel added, her own experience at the hostess stand giving weight to her words. "And if he cares for you as much as you do for him, then what's standing in your way is nothing but air and gossip."

Their encouragement felt like a cool breeze against the stifling heat of fear and doubt. Muriel allowed herself a small smile, the idea of defying convention less daunting with her friends by her side.

"Perhaps you're right," she admitted, warmth blooming in her chest. The thought of William, with his gentle gray eyes and kind words, made her feel brave. "Maybe it is time to cast off these lines of expectation and set sail toward my own happiness."

"Exactly!" Frieda cheered. "Write that letter, Muriel. Let your heart speak through your pen."

"Be bold," Mabel seconded, her spirit of adventure sparking in her eyes. "Chart a course for love, and we'll be here, your steadfast crew."

"Thank you," Muriel replied, her voice gaining strength. "I have been so caught up in the 'shoulds' and 'should nots' that I almost forgot who I am." She straightened in her chair, feeling as though she were shedding old skin, ready to embrace the woman she was becoming. "Fear will not hold me back. I am going to fight for my happiness," she declared, her determination crystallizing with each syllable.

The room hummed with the spirit of rebellion and the alliance of the three young women against the weight of societal expectations. History books might overlook them, but they would write the legacy through their courageous choices and strong friendship.

"Look at you, Muriel Victorine Russell," Frieda exclaimed with a wink. "Ready to conquer the world, or at least Key West."

"Or, more importantly, William's heart," Mabel chimed in.

Muriel allowed herself a small, defiant smile. Yes, she thought, I am ready. With Frieda and Mabel by her side, she felt unstoppable.

CHAPTER 6

Albert Pinder's gaze followed Muriel Russell. Inspecting crates at the dock of the Santos cigar factory, she moved with a grace that seemed to defy the sweltering heat of Key West. Her soft tan complexion was a stark contrast to the rugged seamen and sun-bleached wooden boxes.

After finishing school at age thirteen, Albert had begun working for the wreckers on the island, those who salvaged ships wrecked through storms and misfortune. He had made lots of friends among the seamier island traders. As soon as he earned money, though, he spent it. Not a single penny could he save to even contemplate supporting a wife, but he was ignoring that right now.

At eighteen, Albert was now a big-shouldered, burly lad with dark brown eyes. His black hair was cropped short and his skin was darkened by years of exposure to the tropical sun. His manners were just above acceptable, even in his mother's eyes. His father had tried to groom him for "fine society" and a career in the family business, but Albert just was not interested. Albert had defied his parent's latest attempt to get him a respectable career with one of the locally owned businesses. Instead, he had joined the maritime services. His goal was to prove his worth as Muriel's future spouse.

Albert leaned against the weather-worn railings of the SS *Mascotte* where he worked as a new deckhand. He had taken this job just to be close to Muriel as this ship came into Key

West often. He watched, his eyes narrowing, as Second Officer Roberts approached her.

"Miss Russell, these manifests need your approval," William said.

"Thank you, Mr. Roberts," Muriel replied.

Albert noted that her blue eyes flickered with a warmth she did not show just anyone. From his vantage point, Albert observed the subtle exchange of smiles, the lingering looks that lasted a moment too long. The suspicion that had been gnawing at him now seemed to grow, mocking his naivety. How could he have missed this? The signs were as clear as the Caribbean waters he had sailed since childhood.

Albert fumbled with the coiled rope in his hands, his thoughts a tumultuous sea. William, with his respected position as the ship's second officer, stood tall and confident beside Muriel. Albert could not help but compare his own stature as an apprentice to William's seasoned poise. He felt a boy playing at a man's work, while William ... William was the sort of man that fathers would want their daughters to marry.

"Betrayed by a Bahamian," Albert muttered under his breath. A bitter taste rose in his mouth.

"Say something, Pinder?" one deckhand called out, jolting Albert back to the present.

"Nothing," he snapped, sharper than intended. The deckhand shrugged and turned away, leaving Albert to stew in his thoughts.

Jealousy seared through Albert, like the midday tropical sun, as he watched William place a hand on Muriel's back, guiding her away from the bustle of the dock to a quieter spot between stacks of cargo. There, shielded from prying eyes, the laugh they shared felt like a punch to Albert's gut. Rage simmered within him, fueled by visions of what could happen in those hidden moments.

"Who does he think he is?" Albert whispered to himself, his knuckles whitening around the railing. He was no stranger to hard work, but seeing Muriel with William made all his efforts seem inconsequential. He was ready to cast off his father's disapproval and make a name for himself.

Albert had hoped—had foolishly believed—that Muriel might look past his humble beginnings and see the man he was becoming. Could have been me making her smile like that, he thought. But the fantasy crumbled with each soft exchange between Muriel and William, leaving Albert with a hollow ache of inadequacy.

"They will pay," Albert vowed, the words slipping out like a dark promise. He would expose their forbidden romance. She was betrothed to him. His father had told him that years ago. She should not be carrying on as if she was not already spoken for. Granted, there had been no contact between them since they had left school, but there was that family promise, a contract of marriage, now that they were both eighteen. He would crush her hopes if he could not have her for himself.

Albert closed in on the secret couple, his determined footsteps echoing like a resounding battle cry. Muriel and William, lost in conversation not noticing his approach.

"Enjoying the fine weather, are we?" Albert's voice cut through the air, a deceptive calm masking the turmoil within him.

Muriel turned, her eyes wide with surprise. "Albert! What brings you here?"

"Curiosity," Albert replied, locking eyes with William. "And concern, I suppose."

"Concern?" William's brow furrowed as his gray eyes met Albert's gaze calmly.

"Albert, if this is about your father's shipments—" Muriel began, but Albert cut her off.

"No, Muriel, it's not about my father's shipments. It's about you and—him." He spat the last word out as if it were venom on his tongue. "I know about the little romance you've been hiding."

"Albert, please," Muriel said, her voice a mixture of warning and plea.

"Please what, Muriel? Please pretend I do not see the way he looks at you? Or the way you blush when he is near? Please ignore the betrayal to your family, to—"

"Betrayal?" William interjected, his tone stern. "Our feelings for each other are no one's business but our own."

"Feelings?" Albert scoffed. "You call it feelings? I call it deceit. And I will not stand for it."

"Albert, you are speaking nonsense," Muriel protested, though her complexion had paled.

"Am I?" Albert advanced a step, his anger rising like the tide. "I have seen enough. Heard enough. And I will see that everyone else does as well."

"Are you threatening us?" William asked, squaring his shoulders.

"Consider it a promise," Albert shot back. "Your forbidden romance will be the talk of Key West by nightfall. Let us see how our families take to the news. Our families will be shocked that you have taken up with an outsider." He spat.

WHERE TRADE WINDS MEET

"Think of what you are doing, Albert," Muriel said, her voice steady but tinged with urgency. "This could destroy more than just ... me."

"Maybe it should," Albert retorted. "If we are not meant to be, then perhaps it is justice that this little dalliance ends."

"Justice?" Muriel echoed, her blue eyes glistening with unshed tears. "What justice is there in destroying what little happiness I have found?"

"Justice for every man who stands in the shadows while another takes what is not rightfully his," Albert declared. "Justice for me."

"Albert!" Muriel pleaded, extending her trembling hand. "There has to be another way."

"Another way would have been honesty," Albert said, stepping away from her touch. "But that ship has sailed. Prepare yourselves. The storm is coming."

With that, Albert turned on his heel, leaving behind the shattered silence of two lovers facing the tempest of exposure.

Muriel led William to her office in the back of the factory and closed the door. The sunlight filtered through drawn curtains. She had not noticed the workers who looked up in surprise at her hasty entrance with a man in tow. She paced the length of her office, the hem of her long, cotton skirt whispering across the scarred wooden floor. Pushing the curtains aside in agitation, Muriel took a few deep breaths as she gazed out at the calm sea, so at odds with the storm brewing in her heart.

"William," she began, her voice a whisper. "What if Albert truly goes through with this threat?" Her hands clutched at the windowsill, knuckles whitening.

"First, I would like to understand why this Albert has a claim on you."

She paused to think. She had forgotten that Albert had held this absurd notion of their betrothal since childhood. She had only been worried that her Cuban and Conch families would disapprove of her having a relationship with a royal British Bahamian. Their rivalry among the island people have been off and on again since before the Revolutionary War and with each skirmish since then it has gotten a little worse each year. As she explained about the family contract when they were children, William relaxed a little.

"Then we face it together," William said, his shoulders relaxing as he wrapped his hands around hers and drew her around to face him. "We knew there would be obstacles, Muriel."

"Obstacles, yes," she admitted, "but not ..." Her voice trailed off as she considered the magnitude of their predicament.

"Exposure," he finished for her, the word heavy between them.

"Your position on the *Mascotte*, your reputation—it could all be dashed upon the rocks," Muriel fretted. Her mind raced with the gossipy headlines that might soon splash across the front pages of Key West's newspapers. Every Conch family knew of the family marriage contracts. She did not acknowledge them because she and her friends thought it was an outdated custom. However, her father's reputation and their family business would take a hit as he was expected to honor this contract as he would any business one. Now they would learn about Williams' British Bahamian ties.

"And your family," William added, reaching out to lay a comforting hand on her shoulder. "Your father's standing in the community, your brother's future prospects ... I cannot bear the thought of causing their downfall."

"Nor I," she murmured. She leaned into his touch despite the fear gnawing at her insides. "I have not even thought about your own family. What would they think of me?"

He sighed, a sound that seemed to carry the weight of the ocean itself. "My family has their heir and should not be upset by whom I choose to spend my life with. But our dreams may have to wait. If Albert speaks true, our journey might end before it even begins."

Muriel turned to face him. Her eyes met his with a steely determination that belied her earlier uncertainty. "We cannot let fear and implied expectations change our course. We chose love, William, despite our family's conventions and desires for our future that would keep us apart. Are we to abandon ship at the first sign of rough seas?"

"No," he answered firmly. His hand moved from her shoulder to cradle her cheek. "No, we hold fast. But we must consider every possibility, prepare for the worst while hoping for the best."

"Hope is a lantern in the dark," she quoted. Her mother had often recited this saying in times of trouble. "Let us keep it well lit, then," she said with more conviction as she smoothed traces of worry from her face and tucked her hair back into its prim bun.

"Indeed," William agreed. A small, wistful smile graced his lips. "For without hope, what are we but sailors adrift, with neither a compass nor a star to guide us?"

"Then we navigate this storm," Muriel resolved, her own smile an echo of his. "Together."

"Always," he vowed.

⁂

As the setting sun cast a warm glow over the docks, Muriel and William approached the wharf where the *Mascotte* was moored. Albert paced the deck in agitation, slamming his right fist into his left hand as he mumbled to himself. He had his back toward the approaching couple.

"Albert," Muriel's steady, clear voice cut through the salty air,. "We need to talk."

He spun around. At the sight of them standing there together—united and resolute—his expression hardened.

"Talk?" Albert scoffed bitterly. "What is there to talk about? I have seen enough."

"Then you have seen how much we care for each other," William replied, stepping forward. Despite the calm he projected, his hand trembled in Muriel's.

"Love does not give you the right to deceive everyone," Albert shot back, his gaze flitting between them.

"Nor does it give you the right to play judge," Muriel countered, her blue eyes unwavering. "We are not here to argue. We are here to tell you that your threats will not sway us."

WHERE TRADE WINDS MEET

"Is that so?" Albert's lips curled into a sneer. "Then you will throw away your reputations to break Muriel's contract with my family?"

"Yes," William said. "This is a new century. Muriel is not bound by a childhood betrothal."

"For heaven's sake, Albert. I have not seen you since you finished school. We have not spent any time together and certainly you have not courted me." Muriel's voice cracked with the intensity of frustration.

"You were given to me!" Albert's eyes narrowed. "Our families made a contract, and it remains binding."

"No, Albert. I do not belong to anyone but myself," Muriel said firmly. "I will remind my father of that again when he returns from his business trip next week." She squeezed William's hand. "Love is a leap of faith, and we jumped together."

"Then prepare to reap the whirlwind," Albert growled. He turned and stormed away, his threat hanging in the air like a gathering storm.

As they watched him go, Muriel and William knew the time would come very soon to face her family.

CHAPTER 7

Key West, a gem of an island perched at the tip of Florida, embraced a history that blended cultures like the vibrant threads of a Bahamian quilt. The trade winds had built the town's foundation, as Bahamian immigrants infused their indomitable spirit into its sandy streets and conch houses. These settlers from the sea brought with them a legacy of resilience and a flair for maritime commerce that became the pulse of Key West.

William Roberts, with gray eyes steady as a ship's compass, knew the waters between Nassau and this sun-washed isle like the lines on his own sun-bronzed hands. As the *Mascotte* cut through the azure waves, he stood watch, second officer to none but the sea itself. His Bahamian heritage marked him as much as the light-brown hair that caught the sun's kiss, branding him an outsider to some, yet an integral thread in Key West's vibrant tapestry.

Just ashore, Muriel Russell, the head shipping agent for the Santos cigar factory, surveyed the bustling port with an eagle's precision. Her gaze, the sharp blue of the ocean at dawn, missed nothing. Born and bred in Key West, she was tall and carried herself with an air that defied the corseted expectations placed upon her slender frame. Her hat was neatly pinned to her light-brown hair, though a few rebellious strands danced in the sea breeze, as untamed as her spirit.

Their worlds, while revolving around the same sun of maritime tradition, were governed by societal norms as inflexible as the hulls of the ships they both held dear. William, with his lineage tracing back to the earliest British settlers in the Bahamas, straddled two realms. Although accepted for his nautical prowess, he was held at arm's length when moored to the dock. Muriel, meanwhile, navigated the male-dominated world of shipping with a poise that belied the undercurrent of resistance she faced daily.

"Mr. Roberts!" called out a *Mascotte* deckhand. "We'll be docking shortly."

"Thank you, Jenkins," William replied, his voice carrying the lilt of his homeland. He scanned the horizon, noting Muriel's familiar silhouette standing resolute against the port's chaos. Their eyes met across the expanse of water and wharf, a silent acknowledgment of the challenges each morning brought.

"Good day, Miss Russell," William greeted her once ashore. He tipped his cap—a gesture of respect that crossed any divide.

"Mr. Roberts," Muriel responded with a nod, her tone warm yet professional. "The shipment arrived on schedule; I presume?"

"Indeed," he affirmed. "You'll find everything in order, as always."

Their conversation flowed with the ease of two souls who shared more than just transactions of cargo and manifests. Each word, each glance exchanged, was fraught with their unspoken bond—a connection nurtured not only by shared ambitions but also by the courage to dream beyond the constraints of their time.

WHERE TRADE WINDS MEET

As William returned to his duties aboard the *Mascotte* and Muriel to her ledgers and lists in her office at the factory.

Later that evening, Muriel fanned herself lightly as she stepped into the parlor where her mother sat embroidering by the window. The atmosphere was thick with anticipation of confrontation, a situation all too familiar in the Russell household.

"Your brother tells me you were speaking to that British Bahamian sailor again," her mother began, not looking up from her needlework. Each stitch was a silent indictment.

"William is the second officer on the *Mascotte*, Mother. It is my job to interact with him." Muriel's voice was steady despite the flutter in her chest.

"Yes, interact but there's talk, Muriel. People see more than just business in your eyes."

"Let them talk. My conscience is clear." Her chin lifted, though her heart raced like the wings of a caged hummingbird.

"Conscience will not shield you from whispers or protect our name," her mother retorted. She met Muriel's gaze with a look that seemed to say love was a luxury they could ill afford.

Across town, William faced his own inquisition amid the salty timbers of the crew quarters aboard the SS *Mascotte*.

"Bill, ya courtin' trouble with that island girl," Jenkins cautioned, his accent a comforting echo of home.

"She's more than that, Jenkins. She sees beyond the horizon, like we do," William defended, eyes ablaze with an emotion he dared not voice.

"Her family has strong ties to this place, like the roots of the mangroves, Ours are elsewhere," Jenkins replied, turned and walked away satisfied that he said his peace.

William just harrumphed and moved over to lean against the ship's railing gazing out over the bustling city deep in thought.

On shore, the streets of Key West teemed with life, a mosaic of colors and sounds that blended like the waters of the Gulf and the Atlantic. Fruit vendors hawked their wares in singsong voices, while children darted between stalls, their laughter rising above the clatter of horse-drawn carriages. The scent of frying conch mingled with the tang of salt and tobacco, weaving an intoxicating spell unique to this corner of the world.

Yet for all its vibrancy, the town bore an undercurrent of unspoken rules, invisible lines drawn in the sand. People like William and Muriel dared to blur these lines with every stolen glance, every word charged with hidden meaning. They moved through the bustling crowds, each absorbed in their duties, aware of the gulf between them, a gulf wider than the Florida Straits. Their shared defiance was as subtle as the spiced notes carried on the trade winds—present, persistent, but never acknowledged.

WHERE TRADE WINDS MEET

Muriel leaned against the warm bricks of the Santos cigar factory, watching the white plumes of steam from the arriving steamships blend with the indigo sky. The distant clangs and whistles spoke of Henry Flagler's Overseas Railroad, a steel serpent that had brought change to Key West as surely as the tides shifted its sands. The year was 1912, and the world stood on the brink of modernity.

William had arrived to see his beloved looking forlorn. He eased up beside her and pressed his back to the factory wall. Each was silent in their thoughts as they watched people hustling purposely in the afternoon light. "Will," Muriel finally whispered, as she turned her sad eyes upon him. "Do you think it will ever be simpler?"

William turned his solemn eyes to meet hers. "Simpler?" He chuckled without humor. "When has love ever been simple, Muriel?"

Her sigh was lost amid the rattle of carriage wheels on brick, "I mean, with all this progress ... the railroad connecting us to Miami, the rest of the states .... You would think people would be more open-minded."

"Progress in industry does not always mean progress in thought," William remarked, glancing around to ensure their conversation remained private. "This town thrives on the tobacco we bring in, yet still clings to old norms like barnacles to a ship's hull."

"Sometimes I dream of a place where it is just us, where no one cares you came from Nassau, or that I am not what they expect me to be," Muriel confessed. Her blue eyes betrayed the weariness that painted her lightly tanned skin.

"These islands are our home, true," William replied, his voice tinged with frustration. "It is where my family found hope after leaving England, where your father built his legacy. Can we abandon it for a dream?"

"Maybe dreams are worth chasing," she countered, her determination flaring. "Especially when reality keeps trying to smother them."

"Perhaps," he admitted, a longing note threading through his words. "But, for now, we have responsibilities here, Muriel. My position on the *Mascotte*, your role here at the factory ... We are each part of something bigger."

"Being part of something bigger does not mean we have to be smaller," she shot back, her gaze fierce. "There has to be room for us, too. For our love."

"Soon, my love," he said. With hope in his voice, he added, "One day, Key West will be known not just for Flagler's railroad or your cigars, but for being a place where two people can choose their own path."

"Until then, we fight?" Muriel asked, her voice steady.

"Until then, we fight," William confirmed, his smile warming her within. "Together."

Unseen by the couple, Albert Pinder lurked and seethed, hidden by the stacks of boxes ready for shipping to the cigar factory's customers. Although he had not told her parents about Muriel's tryst with the sailor yet, he was working on a permanent solution to his problem.

WHERE TRADE WINDS MEET

The next day the couple had agreed to meet on the less traveled Simonton Street for a late picnic lunch. They did not have a lot of time before they had to tell Muriel's father about their romance. William leaned against the rough bark of a mahogany tree, watching as Muriel approached through the dappled sunlight of the Key West afternoon. The town's bustle seemed to quiet in her presence, the air itself holding its breath as she moved with the grace of the ocean waves he knew so well. He noticed that she had some kind of metal-looking box in her hand.

Smiling up at William, Muriel opened the metal box she was carrying and pulled forward the round lens section. "I borrowed this from a friend at the newspaper office. She says it is called a Kodak Vest Pocket Camera. She showed me how to take a picture. It seems to be quite easy. I would like to take a picture of you before you ship out again."

"Well, keep smiling at me like that and I will do anything you wish." William stood up straight smiling back at Muriel seeing the tip of her tongue clamped between her lips as she concentrated on the task before her.

Looking through the little window as she had been instructed, she found William and pressed the button. Smiling triumphantly, she laughed and pushed the new little machine back into its box. This she tucked into the pocket on the side of her skirt to return to her friend to have the picture developed. She loved all the new technology that was reaching the islands.

"Escape with me," she whispered, reaching for his hand. Her fingers were a lifeline amid the swirling currents of disapproval they faced each day.

"Only if it is to the end of the world," William replied, the corners of his mouth lifting in a half smile. They both knew their world ended at the water's edge, but in each other's company, it felt infinite.

They walked down to a quiet cove away from the main streets and onto a sandy shore, away from prying eyes and harsh whispers. Here, they were two souls cast adrift, finding harbor in one another.

"Sometimes I feel we are living in another time," she mused, tracing patterns in the sand with her toe. "A time when our love is not a scandal."

"Perhaps we are ahead of our time," he mused, looking out at the sea. Their hands remained clasped, a silent vow against the tide of tradition that sought to pull them apart.

"Like the spongers," Muriel said, gesturing toward the distant boats with their sails unfurled, "we dive deep, hoping to surface with something precious. Something worth the risk."

"Love is always worth the risk," William affirmed.

"Muriel!" The shrill sound of her name shattered their moment of peace. Her younger brother, Bryan, strode toward them, his face twisted in frustration.

"Father's looking for you!" he announced, not bothering to hide his disapproval. "You do not get paid to dawdle on the beach."

"Nor do I get paid to listen to your lectures," Muriel retorted, standing her ground while William watched, his jaw set.

"Is this what you want?" her brother continued, nodding scornfully toward William. "To throw away your good name for him?"

WHERE TRADE WINDS MEET

"Her name is hers to use as she sees fit," William interjected, stepping forward. "Just as my heart is mine to give to whom I choose."

"Enough!" Muriel cut in before her brother could reply. "I am not property to be bartered or judged."

"Choices have consequences, Muriel," Bryan Russell warned darkly before turning on his heel and leaving them alone once more.

"Does it ever get easier?" she asked, searching William's eyes for reassurance.

"Each day with you is easier than a lifetime without," he answered truthfully, drawing her into an embrace that spoke of strength forged in adversity.

And with the sun beginning to moved closer to the horizon, painting the sky with hues of defiance, they shared a quiet kiss to seal the night and their convictions. William reluctantly pulled away, "I am sorry to say I cannot accompany you to meet your father this afternoon. My captain has made arrangements to sail with the tide this evening as we have a run up the coast to the Carolinas. I do not know how soon we will return."

Putting her fingers to his lips Muriel whispered, "Do not worry about me. Please, keep yourself safe and return to me as quickly as you are able."

Still holding her arms he explained, "The captain received a telegram from the New York office. Early winter storms may make their way as far south as North Carolina. We have been tasked with delivering as much fresh fruit and other supplies to their main train depot up north as quickly as possible."

Reaching up, Muriel gave William a quick kiss, then turned and walked toward the main street to catch the next trolley home.

William watched her go, hoping for one quick glance back at him. When she was out of sight, he sprinted toward the docks to board his ship and take up his duties once more.

CHAPTER 8

Hunched over a chart on the bridge of the SS *Mascotte*, Second Officer William Albert Roberts traced the ship's course with a finger as he looked for faster routes back to the Keys. Their business in the Carolinas had taken longer than expected, requiring him to work extra shifts when some of the seamen did not return after their last shore run. He did not know what had happened to those men, but the ship's departure could not be delayed just for a few missing crew members.

A little later, William's hands were steady on the ship's wheel despite the exhaustion tugging at his muscles. He didn't mind the fatigue; it was a small price to pay for the shared dreams of a home somewhere in the United States. He smiled at the memory of Muriel and her talk of travel on the high seas. Little did she know yet of the work involved in keeping these ships afloat, their passengers happy, and the cargo delivered in a timely manner.

A sudden commotion startled him out of his reverie. It began as a distant clamor, swelling into a cacophony of shouts with the unmistakable sound of booms from cannon fire that, thankfully did not hit its mark. William's heart skipped a beat, not from romance this time, but from raw alarm.

Pirates.

They seem to materialize from the mist like specters, their sails a foreboding black against the pale morning sky. The crew's usual chatter stopped and was replaced by urgent cries. The pirates' ship slammed up alongside of the *Mascotte*. Those wily men were swinging over on ropes that had been arrowed into and around the *Mascotte's* rigging. They boarded with the ferocity of a hurricane hitting the coast. Swords flashed and pistols barked orders louder than any thunderstorm.

"Secure the deck!" yelled a voice, harsh and commanding. More invaders swarmed aboard, their presence an affront to the *Mascotte's* peace.

Pandemonium reigned. Passengers screamed and scrambled for cover. Crew members were rounded up like fish in a net.

"Take everything you can!" one pirate bellowed. Smiling cruelly, he waved a cutlass. His eyes, cold and predatory, swept over the deck, taking in the fear, the confusion, and the treasures ripe for plundering.

William's thoughts flew to Muriel. Her image was a beacon in the chaos. His resolve hardened; these brigands would not dictate their fate,

The SS *Mascotte*, hours earlier a proud vessel of commerce between the islands, was now a floating fortress under siege. Its fate hung in the balance as surely as William's own. With every shout and clash of steel, the dream he had built with Muriel seemed farther away, lost amid the shouts of men who knew only greed and violence.

William's heart hammered against his ribs. The chaos of the ship being overrun threatened to overwhelm his senses, but he clung to clarity with a grip as sure as the one he had held on the ship's wheel. As the pirates brandished their weapons with brutish glee, William's mind raced through the drills they had practiced for such dreaded eventualities. He needed to be the calm in the storm for his crew.

"Stow away! Hide where you can," he commanded, his voice low and urgent. He scanned the disarray for an opportunity. His fellow seafarers, recognizing the authoritative timbre despite the undercurrent of peril, nodded and dispersed like shadows flitting through the narrowing corridors of safety.

William briefly observed their retreat, then ducked behind a bulkhead. He pressed himself against the cool metal as vibrations of heavy boots thudded ever closer. The truth was unavoidable; he was going to be captured.

"Where's your captain?" a pirate growled, grabbing a young deckhand by the collar. "Speak, or it'll be the plank for ya!"

The threat of violence was tangible. William knew the gravity of their situation. The ransom these sea marauders would demand could be more than just gold—it could cost them their lives.

"Captain's indisposed," William called out, emerging from his cover with hands raised in feigned surrender. "I'm Second Officer Roberts. What do you want?"

"Smart man," sneered the pirate leader, a hulking figure with a scar running like a riverbed across his cheek. "We want everything this tub's got—gold, goods, the lot. And for insurance, we'll be needing hostages. You'll do for starters."

The assailant pointed a pistol at William, its threat a silent scream. Menace emanated—not only from the cold metal but also from the malice in the raider's eye. His look promised torment if his desires were not met.

"Take me, then," said William. His even tone betrayed none of the fear clawing at his insides. "But know this—Key

West does not take kindly to thieves. You will have the entire island's chain upon you soon enough."

"We will see about that, Mr. Officer. Secure him!" Laughter erupted among the pirates, bitter and mocking.

As rough hands seized him, William's thoughts spiraled to Muriel. His resolve to return to her safe and sound became a silent vow, fueling his courage like a wind into sails. Whatever it took, he'd weather this tempest for her. On the pirate's deck, he stood at attention with his hands tied behind his back, his heart throbbing, as he watched the crew move the last of the cargo and set the *Mascotte* adrift to founder wherever it would.

The ripples of panic had barely spread across Key West when the news was telegraphed to the magistrate, who then telephoned the harbor master. At the cigar factory, Muriel received a call from an uncle who worked in the harbor master's office. The words "SS *Mascotte*" and "pirates" crashed into her world with the force of a rogue wave, leaving her breathless.

Frieda came bursting into her office and grabbed her in a tight hug. "I just heard from my cousin at the magistrate's office." She stepped back to look into Muriel's shell-shocked face and then pulled her into another hug.

"William," Muriel whispered, her wide blue eyes storming with fear. Her hands clenched into fists, the knuckles white and clutching her friend's back. Pulling herself from the embrace, she shuddered, took a deep breath and demanded, "What do you know?"

WHERE TRADE WINDS MEET

"It was pirates. They took most of the cargo, a couple of passengers and crew as hostages, and set the ship adrift. We only know about it this quickly because there was another ship on the scene within the hour of the attack and they found some of the hidden crew and the sick captain, tied up but alive. One of the hostages is your William."

"It cannot be true," she murmured. But the sinking feeling in her gut told her otherwise. William was out there, somewhere beyond the familiar shores, his life dangling on the whim of ruthless marauders.

"William is strong," she said aloud, her voice steadying as the initial shock gave way to resolve. "He will hold on. And we will bring him back."

Frieda nodded, her own determination mirroring Muriel's. "What do we do? How can we help?"

"We start by not losing our heads," Muriel replied. She pulled herself up to her full height, her lightly tanned skin now flushed with purpose. "I need to know everything—where, how many, what weapons. We need a plan."

"Let's fetch Mabel," Frieda suggested, already halfway to the door. "She's at the restaurant, but she'll drop everything for this."

"Good thinking," Muriel agreed. She followed Frieda out into the balmy Key West air. "We need all the help we can get."

The two women moved with haste, their skirts swishing against their legs as they hurried through the bustling streets. They found Mabel arranging menus by the hostess stand. Her youthful features lit up at the sight of her friends before she registered the urgency in their demeanor.

"Something's happened," Mabel said, instantly alert.

"It's William," Muriel said, dispensing with pleasantries. The *Mascotte* crew is in the hands of pirates.

"Lord, have mercy," Mabel gasped, "What will you do?"

"Whatever it takes," Muriel answered. "Frieda, go to your father's store. See if he has heard anything about the pirates' whereabouts or plans. Mabel, you ask around here. The sailors love to talk. Maybe someone's seen something that could give us a lead."

"What about you?" Frieda asked, her face lined with worry.

"I'm going to rally every resource I have. My brother knows other sailors and a few captains. We have some other family and more people at the cigar factory who may have information. Both sides of the family have great connections with all the seagoing vessels. Someone must know a way to approach these devils." Her unwavering tone bolstered her friends' spirits like a beacon.

"Be careful," Mabel warned, her eyes reflecting the gravitas of their undertaking.

"Careful will not bring William home," Muriel replied. Her eyes glinted with steely blue resolve. "But bravery just might."

With that, the three women split up, each embarking on their mission to peel back the layers of rumor and hearsay that shrouded the fate of the *Mascotte's* crew. Muriel walked briskly back toward the shipping office, her mind whirring with strategies and contingencies. William admired her tenacity, her refusal to bend to society's restrictive norms. Now, she would channel that same fire to forge a path through whatever trials lay ahead.

WHERE TRADE WINDS MEET

"Wait for me, William," she whispered into the sea breeze. "I am coming for you."

Muriel paced the floorboards of her modest office, her heels clicking a staccato rhythm that matched the racing of her heart. With each turn, she confronted the photograph she had taken when William was last in port. She had it on her desk, under glass in a wood frame her brother had made. William's eyes seemed to implore her. The news of the kidnapped crew gripped her chest like a vice, but it was the thought of William in danger that squeezed the air from her lungs.

"No!" she whispered. William cannot be killed now that she has found him. Pulling herself up straight a very determined look shone through her eyes. The Muriel Victorine Russell, who had navigated the male-dominated shipping industry with an iron will, would not falter now, not when the man she loved needed her most.

"Think, Muriel, think!" she muttered, her mind a whirlwind of strategy and scenarios. Hope flickered within her, stubborn and defiant, guiding her through the darkness of doubt.

"Alright, ladies," Muriel announced later that evening. She stood tall in Frieda's living room, where she had convened an emergency meeting with her closest allies. "We have a plan."

Frieda and Mabel sat forward earnestly, ready to cast aside their dreams of summer flirtations for a cause far greater.

"Firstly, we need to understand the pirates' movements. They're bold but not unpredictable," Muriel said, unfurling a nautical chart across the coffee table. Her finger traced the routes frequented by the pirates.

"Then what?" Frieda asked, her voice a mix of fear and excitement.

"Then we exploit their patterns," Muriel stated. She pointed to a cove that was rumored to be a pirate hideout. "We lay a trap."

"Is it safe?" Mabel interjected, concern clear in her tone.

"Safe as a moonless night on open waters," Muriel replied with a grim smile. "Which is to say, not at all. But it is our best shot."

"Okay, so we set this trap—but how do we even get close to them without being spotted? Or worse, caught?" Frieda's brow furrowed as she voiced the question that loomed over them.

"Here's where it gets interesting," Muriel said, her blue eyes gleaming with a mix of mischief and resolve. "We will need a boat, one nimble enough to navigate these waters without drawing attention."

"Where are we going to get a boat like that?" Skepticism laced Mabel's words.

"Leave that to me," Muriel assured her. "My brother Bryan has agreed to help us now. He has made some helpful friends over the last two summers working at the docks and I am certain he can help us find something suitable."

"Alright then," Frieda summoned courage that seemed to swell beyond her years. "We have got ourselves a pirate hunt."

WHERE TRADE WINDS MEET

"Indeed," Muriel nodded. "We will need to be quick and quiet. We should approach under the cover of darkness, cut their anchor lines, create a diversion ..."

"Diversion?" Mabel echoed, alarm creeping into her voice.

"Nothing dangerous," Muriel reassured her. "Just enough to draw them out while we search for William."

"Rescuing William from a band of pirates in the dead of night," Frieda mused, with a hint of a grin breaking through. "If this were any other circumstance, it might actually sound thrilling."

"Thrilling or terrifying," Muriel conceded, folding the chart with a decisive snap. "But necessary. For love, for justice, for our future. We cannot allow fear to dictate our fate."

"Here is to bravery then," Mabel said, lifting an imaginary toast, her hostess charm resurfacing.

"To bravery," Frieda echoed, her voice steady and sure.

Muriel nodded, feeling a surge of solidarity with her companions.

In the boat shed next to the docks, Muriel's hands were steady as she tied the last knot, securing a canvas bag filled with supplies and makeshift weapons. There was no time to waste. Her every movement was swift and purposeful. Frieda passed her a coil of rope while Mabel stuffed a small sack with dried meats and fruits. The ticking clock underscored the urgency of their preparations. They had dressed in loose-fitting pantaloons, black as the night, and snug cotton shirts, also black. Each had bound up her hair in a dark kerchief. Having been raised on these islands, all three knew how to handle a blade and protect themselves.

"Remember, we might have to bribe some of these ruffians for information," Muriel said. Her eyes betrayed none of the apprehension that tightened in her chest. "Gold coins, jewelry—anything you can spare."

"Done," Frieda replied. She slipped a few heirloom rings off her fingers and into the bag, the weight of her family legacy now repurposed for the daring rescue.

"Here," Mabel added, tucking a flask of rum between the folds of cloth. "This might loosen a few tongues, or at least distract them long enough for us to slip by."

"Let us hope it does not come to that," Muriel murmured, though they all knew the odds they were facing.

Bryan was true to his word. As dusk settled over Key West like a shroud, the three women found themselves on a borrowed skiff, the briny scent of the sea mingling with their collective trepidation. Bryan's friends, seasoned by the capricious whims of the ocean, had provided them not just the vessel but also a crudely drawn map marked with areas known for pirate activity.

"Keep your wits about you," one dockhand had warned as they set out. "Them pirates ain't known for their hospitality."

Navigating by the stars, they came upon the faint outline of a large, dark sailing ship in the distance. Muriel took the helm with a confidence she didn't feel.

"Stay low," she instructed, her voice barely audible over the sound of the water and the creaking wood. Frieda and Mabel hunkered down, their eyes scanning the horizon for any sign of unwelcome company.

WHERE TRADE WINDS MEET

"Is that—" Frieda began, pointing toward a flickering light in the distance.

"Another boat or boats," Mabel finished for her, tension knitting her brow.

"Could be fishermen ... or worse," Muriel said, adjusting their course subtly to avoid detection. The skiff rocked as a larger wave rolled beneath them, a reminder of the unrelenting sea that surrounded them.

"Or it could be our chance to find out exactly where they are keeping William," Frieda said, the hint of steel in her tone belying her youthful appearance.

"Either way, we need to be careful," Muriel cautioned. The thrill of the adventure was there—somewhere beneath layers of fear and resolve—but it paled compared to the thought of seeing William again, safe and unharmed.

"Look, there!" Mabel whispered fiercely, pointing toward a dim outline rising and falling with the swells.

Squinting through the darkness, Muriel could make out the shape of another ship. Her breath hitched in her throat as the gravity of their mission crashed over her anew. They had to be close now, close enough to hear the distant shouts of men and the creak of strained ropes.

"Ready yourselves," she said, her grip tightening on the helm. Their plan, reckless as it was, unfurled before them like a sail catching wind. Ahead lay the unknown, fraught with peril and promise. They had turned off the small engine. Frieda and Mabel each took an oar to propel them forward in silence. Each stroke brought them closer to William—and to the defining moment of their lives.

The skiff's prow cut through the inky waters with a determined grace, each stroke of the oars a silent battle cry. Muriel fixed her eyes on the dark, hulking ship, her heart thudding against her ribs like a caged bird desperate for freedom. Beside her, Frieda and Mabel's faces formed grim lines, as they held unwavering resolve like the lighthouse piercing the night behind them.

"Steady," Muriel whispered, her voice louder than the lap of water against wood. "Remember the plan." Unsure whether those coming on the other were friends or foes, the trio decided to climb up on the farthest side of the ship.

Nodding, Frieda and Mabel readied themselves. They clutched makeshift weapons fashioned from shipyard scraps. The bribes and inducements lay forgotten, jumbled in a sack in the skiff's bottom. They were so close now. The pirates' coarse laughter carried over the waves, a jarring reminder of the danger that awaited.

With a last heave, the trio guided the skiff to the shadowed side of the pirate ship. The ropes they'd been told about by their local contacts dangled within reach, the only lifeline between them and William. Muriel was the first to grasp the coarse fibers, pulling herself up with an agility that belied her society upbringing.

"Up you come," she hissed to Frieda and Mabel, who followed suit, ascending the ropes with a grace born of desperation.

On deck, the chaos was palpable. Pirates roamed with careless brutality, drunk and weaving, their cutlasses gleaming under the sparse light of lanterns. Muriel scanned the pandemonium, searching for William's familiar figure.

WHERE TRADE WINDS MEET

"Split up," she instructed tersely. "Find him."

As Muriel ducked behind a crate, the clash of steel rang out, sending a shiver down her spine. Peering around the crate's edge, she saw a pirate brandishing his weapon at a cowering passenger. Her hand tightened around the jagged piece of metal she held—this was not the time for hesitation.

"Hey!" Muriel emerged from her hiding spot, her voice slicing through the tumult. The pirate spun. Surprise etched his weathered face, then contorted into a snarl.

"Where did you come from, little lady?" He advanced, blade at the ready.

"From the depths of the sea to avenge my one true love," Muriel retorted. She dodged as he lunged forward.

The intensity of the struggle was palpable, each movement a precarious dance with mortality as she countered with her rudimentary weapon. From the corner of her eye, she could see Frieda grappling with another assailant, while Mabel unleashed a ferocity that belied her genteel appearance.

"William!" Muriel called out, hoping her voice would reach him, wherever he was.

Suddenly Frieda shouted a warning. A heavy blow sent Muriel staggering. The pirate had caught her off guard. His cutlass glinted ominously above her.

"Give it up, darling," he sneered, poised to strike.

"Never," Muriel gasped, defiance igniting in her veins. But as the blade descended, a figure hurtled from the shadows—a blur of determination and strength.

"William!"

The cutlass clattered to the deck, knocked aside by a forceful blow. William stood there, panting, his gray eyes flashing in the dim light. For a heartbeat, time stood still as they locked gazes, a thousand words passing between them.

"Behind you!" Muriel's warning came just in time as another pirate charged toward William.

Muriel and William fought back-to-back, a seamless unit against the encroaching tide of marauders. Every slash, every parry was a testament to their shared will to survive, to reclaim the life they had planned together.

"Time to end this." Muriel panted, her energy waning though her spirit was undeterred.

"Agreed," William replied, just as a loud boom echoed across the water.

All heads turned to the source of the sound. The distraction gave the beleaguered crew of the SS *Mascotte* the opening they needed. Reinforcements from Key West, alerted by Muriel's allies, approached fast with cannon volleys blazing across the bow of the pirate ship.

"Get down!" William pushed Muriel to the deck as bullets whistled overhead.

In the ensuing mêlée, it was impossible to tell friend from foe. Muriel clung to William, her heart hammering. They spied the outline of the boat of rescuers looming ever closer. It seemed the whole town of Key West was coming to take these pirates down. Muriel and William looked at each other and grinned.

Jumping up, he shouted "Come on!" He and Muriel sliced through the crew's restraints and then the passengers' bonds, urging them to quickly move to the back of the ship.

"Jump!" Mabel shouted as she went over the side of the ship sliding down the rope to their borrowed boat below.

WHERE TRADE WINDS MEET

And so they leaped, hands clasped together, into the abyss below. The chilly embrace of the gulf stream waters enveloped them, muffling the sounds of battle as they kicked toward the surface.

As they broke through the water's grasp, gulping in the salty air, Muriel looked around wildly for her friends. But the smoke from the gunfire obscured her vision, leaving them adrift amid the roiling waves.

"Where are they?" Muriel spluttered, panic rising in her throat.

"Over here!" It was Frieda. She waved from aboard the rescue boat, only yards away.

"Swim!" William shouted.

Coming around the bow of the ship were ten or more other steam powered boats. They had one rescuer aboard ready to pull the victims in and take them to safety. It seemed all the cannon fire had been a distraction to allow the smaller boats to get into place to intercept the hostages and shoot any pirates who had jumped ship. Williams crew and the ship's passengers headed toward the whispering voices out in the water, beckoning them forward away from the pirates.

Everyone had counted off as they rolled into the rescue boats to ensure no passenger or crew member was left behind. Then each of the boat's steam engine was fired up and the little flotilla swiftly moved off back the way they had come. Onboard the main ship was a magistrate and a contingent of US Navy officials, ready to take the pirates into custody and to retrieve whatever was left of *Mascotte's* cargo as it pulled up alongside the pirate ship.

Laughing aloud, each woman gave a big shout. "We did it!" The little craft shook with their enthusiasm. William grabbed Muriel into a tight hug. Her two friends looked at the smiling faces of the crew and passengers, realizing they would live another day.

CHAPTER 9

The waves battered the side of the SS *Mascotte* with a wrathful persistence, as though it sought to take back what the pirates had stolen. Amid the chaos, William stood on the deck, his gaze locked onto the shrinking silhouette of Muriel's lifeboat as it bobbed away through the frothy swells. Her figure, once so close he could count the freckles on her cheeks, was now nothing more than a smudge against the merciless expanse of the sea.

"Mr. Roberts!" a sailor shouted over the storm. William's heart pounded in sync with the crashing waves—a drumbeat of separation.

"William! We need you here!" The urgency in the sailor's voice pierced his dreams. He shook his head to clear it of the images his imagination had created after the dramatic rescue by his beloved and her friends.

"Right, let's secure the damage." William barked orders. He slipped into his role as the second officer with practiced ease, but his mind was adrift, lost in the turbulent wake of his worry-filled dreams. As the crew scrambled to mend sails and patch breaches, William's hands moved, tying knots he could do in his sleep. Yet, every fiber of his being yearned for Muriel—the sound of her laughter, the spark in her blue eyes when she spoke of their future travels.

"Damn it all," he muttered under his breath as a sense of foreboding settled on his chest. Could their dream wither in the face of piracy, pejorative relatives, and other perils? The thought was like a gale-force wind that threatened to topple his resolve.

Later, in the solitude of his quarters, an oil lamp's dim light cast long shadows on the maps sprawled across his desk. He had obtained copies of the maps Muriel had made for herself of where she wanted to go and what she wanted to see. They lay on his table mocking him. The legacies of their two-family clashed and interfered with his dreams. He had never really thought about his ancestry before.

William had grown up on one of the big islands, on a plantation that his family had procured during the reign of the British Empire. Yes, they had freed their slaves years before the Americans had been forced to free theirs, but the British still ruled over those island provinces. It seemed much of the caste system remained in place even into this new twentieth century. Muriel's people were descendants of the first settlers in Key West and of the first of the Cubans to move from their island nation to explore the former Spanish territory of Florida. They stayed through the British occupation and remained when the British fled after the Revolutionary War. The British had returned before the American Civil War and had supported the South in that fight, but they fled again when it ended. It is no wonder her people resented the British Bahamians.

"Is love truly enough?" he whispered into the empty room, his fingers tracing the routes they'd charted. With every port of call, there was an adventure they had plotted, but now doubt crept in like the tide, eroding the shore of his certainty. Could he, a mere officer, and Muriel, a woman with ambitions larger

WHERE TRADE WINDS MEET

than Key West itself, ever bridge the gap between the lives they currently led and the life they envisioned?

"Adventure is a cruel mistress," he said, his voice barely above the howl of the wind outside. He was finally coming to terms with Muriel's heritage and his own. No wonder the British Bahamians always sent their sons and daughters off to England to find wives and husbands. They had to find a way to bridge the divide.

He stood and began pacing the room. Each step was like wading through the shallows of despair. Yet even in his darkest musings, the image of Muriel—brave, unyielding Muriel—stood as a beacon in the fog. She was the compass that gave him direction, the anchor that held him steady amid the storm.

"By the stars, I will not let this be our end," he vowed. The conviction in his voice carved through the uncertainty. Love, he decided, was a vessel resilient enough to carry them through tempests and turmoil, and he would navigate its tumultuous waters until they reached the shores of their dreams, together.

***

Muriel clutched the locket at her throat, a talisman against the dread that rose with each wave. Her fingers traced the contours of the tiny key embossed on its surface, a symbol of the life she and William had yearned to unlock together. The relentless sea stretched between them now, a vast expanse that seemed impassable.

"William," she whispered into the briny air, imagining him standing steadfast on the deck of the *Mascotte*, his gray eyes scanning the horizon for a sign of her. She shook her head, casting away the tendrils of fear that sought to strangle her resolve. "We'll navigate this storm, my love."

Pacing in her office while the winter storm raged outside she too was thinking of her heritage and William's. Why should they have to bow to convention? After all, it was the twentieth century and things were changing all around the country. There was even talk of women fighting to get to vote in elections.

Falling into her office chair in despair, she sent out a silent plea to the seas to be kind to her William and bring him back to her so that they could resolve this quandary and begin their life journey together.

William stood by the railing; eyes fixed on the churning water below. The rhythmic lapping against the ship's side was a mockery of comfort, a reminder of the ebb and flow of hope and despair battling within him this past week at sea.

"Damnation," he muttered, his voice lost to the wind. He pictured Muriel's determined gaze, the way she handled the ledgers and negotiations back at the factory with an ironclad finesse. If anyone could weather this ordeal, it was her.

But what of himself? Torn between duty and desire, William's heart waged its own war. Could he be the partner Muriel deserved?"

'Adventure is a cruel mistress', Muriel had teased him earlier, her blue eyes alight with mischief. Now those words echoed in his mind, a stark reminder of the unpredictability they faced.

"Mr. Roberts," a voice called out, jolting William from his reverie. He turned to face the sailor, nodding curtly. Business then, not sentiment, must govern his actions.

The *Mascotte* pitched as another wave struck her broadside, sending sheets of rain and sea spray across the deck. William clutched a rail, his knuckles white against the tempest's fury, his gray eyes squinting through the torrents. The storm, indifferent to human plight, howled with relentless abandon, its winds weaving a chorus of despair around the beleaguered ship.

"Steady on," he shouted, though the gale swallowed his voice. He could hardly recall a time when the horizon was not obscured by such wrathful skies, turning the once-cerulean blanket into a tapestry of ominous grays.

William fought to keep his footing as another rogue wave crashed over the bow. He recalled the first time he saw Muriel, sitting quietly on the trolley, her blue eyes reflecting the vastness of the ocean. She was like a siren, enchanting him not with a song but with her spirit, her fierce independence.

It was her laughter that echoed in his heart amid the darkness, her smile that cut through the despair.

William gripped the ship's wheel more tightly as a monstrous wave loomed over the bow. He could barely make out the shapes of his crew in the torrential downpour. Each man was a shadow battling the storm's fury. The *Mascotte* groaned and creaked beneath him as it strained against nature's assault.

"Steady as she goes," he muttered to himself, a mantra that felt futile. His gaze flickered to the compass, its needle dancing.

Each time it steadied; William's thoughts drifted to Muriel. She was the true north of his turbulent existence, the guiding star by which he navigated life's uncertainties.

But what if he was not her true north? In the storm's chaos, a nagging voice whispered doubts through the howling wind. Was he worthy of her? Could he, a simple second officer, offer her the world they dreamed of, or would the weight of his inadequacies drag them both into the abyss?

The ship lurched violently, tearing William from his reverie. He redoubled his grip, fighting to keep their course out of the gale in the Atlantic and back to the calmer waters of the Gulf. Yet the tempest within raged fiercer than any gale outside.

Back in the cigar factory, Muriel lovingly smoothed a finger over the image of William. The photograph had captured the moment of William's easy smile, which had warmed her for the last week. Huddled in her office, unable to concentrate on her work, the walls seemed to close in around her, the sound of the rain pounding against the brick-covered warehouse, a relentless drumbeat.

"Am I enough?" she whispered to the image; her voice lost in the cacophony. Her fingers traced the outline of his face, seeking comfort in the familiar contours. She pondered the expectations laid upon her—head shipping agent, daughter, sister—and now, perhaps, William's future wife. Could she be all these things and still hold on to the love that had blossomed in such an unlikely place?

WHERE TRADE WINDS MEET

Muriel's heart ached with longing and doubt. She wrestled with the practicalities of loving a seafarer—the constant departures, the risks, the waiting. Her dreams of standing by his side clashed with the reality of her responsibilities on shore. Love was no shield against the storms of life, and she wondered if their bond could withstand the sacrifices required to nurture it.

"Perhaps we are foolish to want so much," she mused, tucking the photograph away. Her resolve hardened; no matter the cost, she would fight for their shared dreams, even when those dreams seemed as insubstantial as the mist that enveloped the ship.

On deck, William braced himself as another wave crashed over the deck. He watched as the various crew members carried out their duties while balancing their bodies against the to-and-fro of the waves. He watched as crewman Albert Pinder worked his way across the deck—tightening the rigging here and there and checking the hatches to ensure they were sealed—until he moved out of sight toward the back of the boat. William did not really trust that one but he worked hard and the captain had no complaints. Since Pinder's big outburst to Muriel, he had kept a low profile. As a matter of fact, William could not remember seeing Pinder before the pirate attack. He had also been among the missing crewmen during the Carolina trip. It would be wise to keep an eye out for that one for the remainder of the trip.

Turning his back on the deck to look out to the rumbling sea, William sighed to himself once more. He squinted through the salt spray. His vision blurred, but his purpose was clear. With every challenge, he recognized the fortitude that Muriel inspired in him. Their love was a beacon, yes, but also an anchor—a steady presence in the tumultuous seas of doubt.

"Love is not just a fair-weather journey," he reasoned, finding a semblance of peace in the thought. "It's navigating the squalls together."

The ship heaved under William's feet. The recent pirate attack had left the ship wounded but still defiant, much like his own heart in the wake of Muriel's absence. She was ashore, and he at sea; their love was a tenuous thread stretched across the expanse of ocean.

Albert stealthily moved up to the pensive second officer who was deep in thought. Just as William became aware of his presence Pinder shoved the unlucky soul overboard into the roiling sea below.

Quickly looking around, he smiled to himself. Earlier, when the storm had lessened, he had signaled the pirate captain using the wireless device the captain had installed the previous year. Albert's friends, the remaining pirates, were following the *Mascotte*, trailing in its wake to pick up this interloper and ransom him to his British Bahamian family. Albert did not care if William lived or died. Chuckling to himself, he went back to his duties, giving himself time to be on the opposite side of the ship before the "man overboard" alarm was raised.

WHERE TRADE WINDS MEET

Muriel was curled up on the couch in her office of the cigar factory, the photo of William cradled in her hands. Her uncle, Carlos Santos, was supervising the last shipment for the day while she pretended to finish off the ledgers for the month. He did not like doing all that paperwork required by the government and the bank, so he gladly left her alone all day to finish that monthly chore. The scent of tobacco was a constant reminder of the life she was expected to lead—one rooted in trade winds and commerce, not the wild freedom of the seas.

"Speak to me, William," she whispered to his image, as if he could hear her over the miles. "Tell me you have not given up on us. On our dream."

As if in response to her plea, the door creaked open. Muriel hastily tucked the photograph beneath a cushion as her uncle stepped inside. His face was lined with concern.

"My sobrina, you have been cooped up here all day. You need some air, some laughter. The world did not end with that pirate scuffle."

"Did it not, Tio?" Muriel's voice trembled, betraying her inner turmoil. "What if that is just the beginning? What if William and I are never meant to—"

"Shush, now. Do not borrow trouble from tomorrow." Carlos sat beside her, enveloping her hand in his rough cigar-maker's grip. "You two have a rare thing. I see it clear as day. But it is fragile, too. Needs tending, faith."

"Faith feels like a gamble when the stakes are your whole heart," Muriel countered, her resolve wavering.

"Life is a gamble, pequeña. And love? Love is the riskiest bet of all. But who are we if not gamblers at heart?"

Muriel laughed despite herself. It was a small surrender to hope. Her uncle smiled—a silent acknowledgment of his continuing battle to keep his wife alive by seeking the best medical help for her failing kidneys. She was his true love. The one he created songs about as he and the others worked rolling the cigars to perfection to be shipped to the famous doctors and rich people of the north. He had always encouraged Muriel to find her heart mate.

Muriel sat at her writing desk, the candlelight flickering across the page of her journal as she penned her latest epistle. Her blue eyes were determined, reflecting a fire that not even the dampening Key West breeze could extinguish. She wrote with purpose, her fair fingers stained with ink, crafting words that carried her spirit across the ocean's expanse.

She addressed all of her entries to William these days as a kind of love letter. It helped clear all those thoughts rushing around in her head. It would also be a way for her to rally her thoughts and speak her mind and heart when he returned. "Dearest William," she began, "we stand at the crossroads of our lives, where the compass of my heart points unwaveringly to you."

As twilight descended upon the island, a soft knock came at her door. Her brother Bryan entered, bearing a letter with unfamiliar handwriting. Hoping for news of William, Muriel tore open the envelope, then gasped in horror.

CHAPTER 10

The letter Muriel received was from one of the pirates who had escaped from the magistrate. Glen Thomas was an educated man who had turned to a life of piracy. He had grown up a Conch but preferred the seamier sides of the islands as he did not like to work hard. He was a distant cousin of Muriel's family and had heard that Muriel was sweet on the second officer of the *Mascotte*. In his letter, Thomas wrote that Muriel might want to get in touch with the British Bahamian's family. If they ever wanted him to be returned, they must pay a finder's fee. It seemed the pirates had found William floating in the Atlantic and they wanted to be paid for his rescue. After reading such tripe, Muriel summoned her own crew and made a plan.

The tropical sun dipped toward the horizon, casting a warm glow over Key West's bustling streets as Muriel and her two friends met with their local contacts. The two men, known simply as Joe and Benny, were brothers whose reputations for discretion and daring had woven them into the fabric of the island's more covert affairs. They leaned against the weathered wall of an alleyway, their eyes scanning the street with casual vigilance.

"Miss Russell," Joe greeted her, tipping his hat ever so slightly. His gaze never fully left the passersby. "Heard you're looking to pull off something not quite by the books."

"Indeed," Muriel replied, her voice steady despite the fluttering in her chest. "It involves someone very dear to me."

Benny, the younger of the two, flashed a sympathetic smile. "We know about you and the second officer, William. Word gets around. Cannot say I've seen a love hold strong through such trying times."

"Your expertise in ... delicate matters is well known," Muriel said. "I wouldn't entrust this to anyone less capable."

Joe nodded, his expression serious. "Risky situations are our specialty, Miss Russell. You can count on us."

"Then Frieda and Mabel will be in contact to confirm our arrangements," Muriel replied and the party dispersed.

Frieda and Mabel retreated to the relative privacy of a fragrant garden behind the Garfunkels' department store where the air was thick with the scent of blooming jasmine. They perched on a wrought-iron bench, huddled close as they reviewed their audacious plan.

"Even with Joe and Benny on board, there's a lot that could go wrong," Frieda muttered, tucking a stray lock of hair behind her ear.

Mabel bit her lip, her brow furrowed in concentration. "Storms at sea, nosy townsfolk, even the law—if we aren't careful, it could all come crashing down."

"Yet if we do nothing, Muriel loses William forever," Frieda pointed out, her tone resolute. "Can you live with that?"

"Of course not," Mabel exclaimed, her resolve hardening. "Muriel's one of our own. And besides, who doesn't love a good romance? It's worth the risk. We'll see them together again, you'll see."

Their conversation reflected the spirit of the time—a period of great social change when the rigid gender roles bent under the pressure of modernity. In plotting to reunite the two lovers, Frieda and Mabel were defying expectations, embracing the evolving notions of justice and relationships. Their youthful determination was a beacon of hope amid the challenges they faced.

As she awaited the arrival of her young conspirators, Muriel's fingers traced the edge of her aunt's battered old desk, the grain of the wood familiar under her touch. The hum of the Santos cigar factory filtered through the window, a constant reminder of the world that bustled on without regard to heartache or longing.

The door creaked open, and Frieda and Mabel stepped in, their faces alight with a determination that seemed incongruous in the somber office. They approached Muriel, exchanging glances that carried the weight of unspoken plans and shared secrets.

"Okay, we have got everything set up," Frieda announced, her voice a blend of excitement and gravity as she produced a creased paper from her dress pocket. Muriel's eyes flickered to the document, her pulse quickening.

"Joe and Benny have confirmed their part as well," Mabel added, "They have lined up a couple of boats for us that are fast and discreet—perfect for slipping past the patrols."

"According to the boys, the pirates keep a close watch during the day," Frieda stated.

"But at night, only a few guards patrol the perimeter," Mabel added. "Benny said there is a trapdoor in the back, near the storeroom. Could be an escape route if things get out of control."

Frieda unfolded the plan with care, pressing it flat against the desktop. "We've mapped out a route around the reefs—a night run to avoid prying eyes."

Mabel added "Joe said he and Benny will be behind us in another boat as we go ashore to look for William just in case something happens to the first boat."

Muriel leaned forward, studying the marked paths that crisscrossed the chart. The lines were like veins, pulsing with life and promise, yet also fraught with peril. She felt the swell of hope in her chest, an ember reignited by the meticulous care as she and her friends poured over their scheme one more time.

"William ... Is he worth all this? You are certain?" Mable asked, her voicc laced with trepidation.

"Without a shadow of a doubt," Muriel responded, her conviction resonating in the quiet room.

"Besides, love like yours does not come by every day," Frieda said, her smile gentle, yet fierce.

Muriel's hands closed into fists upon the table. The possibility of seeing William again fanned the flames of her resolve. Yet, the risks loomed large—like dark clouds on the horizon threatening to engulf her. The fear of failure, of loss, sent a shiver down her spine.

WHERE TRADE WINDS MEET

"William would move heaven and earth for me," she whispered, as if saying it aloud could make it truer. "I must do no less for him."

"Then it's settled," Frieda declared, her words cutting through Muriel's doubts. "We put our plan in motion tonight."

"Tonight," Muriel repeated, the word tasting of both destiny and danger. She raised her eyes to meet those of her coconspirators, finding solace in their shared conviction.

"Tonight," they affirmed together. Their pact was sealed in the fading light of the setting sun, which cast long shadows across the floorboards and illuminated their faces with the warm glow of camaraderie and the promise of adventure.

As Muriel rose from her seat, the wooden chair legs scraped softly against the floorboards in a quiet testament to her decision. The room seemed to hold its breath; the air was thick with the weight of what they were about to undertake. "We do it," she said, her voice carrying an extra edge of determination, "for William, for us. We take this chance."

Frieda nodded, a fierce gleam in her eye. Mabel straightened her shoulders as if readying herself for battle. They knew the stakes, yet there was unspoken joy in their defiance, a thrill in the orchestration of their clandestine mission.

"Alright, let's go over this one more time," Muriel said, unfurling the crinkled map they had sourced from a local fisherman. Freida and Mable huddled together.

"Mabel, you are on lookout," Muriel stated "and I will meet the boys at the boats."

Mabel nodded, her youthful face set with a seriousness that belied her seventeen years. She would be their eyes and ears, alert to any sign of trouble or unwelcome attention.

"And I'll make sure we have all the supplies," Frieda concluded. "Food, water, and enough fuel to get us there and back again."

"Quickly and quietly, that's how it must be done," Muriel added, folding the map with practiced hands. Her days of overseeing shipments had honed her skills in logistics, and those very skills were now the linchpin of their daring escapade.

"Exactly," Frieda agreed. They split up, each to her respective task, moving through the humid evening with a purpose that felt like a current in the air.

Muriel made her way to the docks, her familiarity with its labyrinthine layout serving her well as she slipped past crates and moorings. She met Joe and climbed into the steam-powered boat.

Meanwhile, Mabel wove through the alleyways, her keen eyes missing nothing. A stray cat darted from shadow to shadow, and she envied its stealth. She perched atop a stack of empty barrels near the designated meeting point at the other end of the wharf, her gaze sweeping the area for any signs of curious sailors or the island's ever-present gossips.

Frieda gathered supplies with a speed born of necessity, her mind racing through a checklist. Canned meats, hardtack, fresh water in sealed containers—every item chosen for utility and longevity. She packed these into sturdy sacks, which she then stowed in a hidden alcove behind her father's store, ready for retrieval.

As the stars peppered the velvet sky, a signal came—a soft whistle, barely distinguishable from the sigh of the evening breeze. It was Mabel, signaling all clear Frieda came over to stand next to her.

WHERE TRADE WINDS MEET

The little steam boat pulled up next to the ladies and Joe got out

"I'll catch up to Benny and we will be right behind you."

The ladies packed away the supplies into the bench box inside the boat and sat down, their actions synchronized by mutual trust and the knowledge that every second mattered. Muriel took the helm, her hands steady as she started the engine, pumping in air to the fire to get the steam going, its gush of vapor could promise the journey ahead.

The boat cut through the water; a phantom vessel guided by the moon's silver path. As Key West receded into the distance, Muriel allowed herself a moment of hope, imagining William's gray eyes lighting up at the sight of her, the reunion that would justify all risks taken.

"Stay focused," Frieda murmured, though her voice held a note of excitement. "We're not through yet."

Muriel nodded, her resolve showing in the firm set of her jaw and a determined look in her eyes. Her body was still and thoughtful. She retraced the whirlwind of recent activity to when she had received that message from her long-distance cousin. In her desperation, she had pleaded with her father, her uncle, and anyone else in power to organize a rescue for William. The dreaded pirates who escaped from the Key West rescuers had kidnapped her beloved for ransom. The pirates had tried to get money from William's parents who refused to pay, not even for their beloved second son. She had learned that her father had persuaded most of the family to invest in the railroad, so their funds were tied up in stock. That was a surprise to her, because she thought the railroad was a novelty, at best, in Key West. With all the hurricanes blasting the island every year or so, a rail line did not seem like a good investment to her. And her meager savings were not enough to cover the bounty, either.

After checking with everyone she knew for more information, Muriel had finally learned that William was being held on a small island off the coast of Cuba. He was reportedly in a small warehouse where disreputable wreckers broke down the ships and sorted the salvaged merchandise.

The boat's engine sputtered, a cough in the night that seized Muriel's heart, bringing her out of her reverie. She pumped the bellows lever up and down urging the engine to come back to life. Puffing out a gasp in protest, the motor fell silent.

"Let me," Frieda said, her fingers deft as she checked the air lines from the coal burner to the steam pump. Her brows knit in concentration under the faint glow of the lantern.

Muriel could feel the minutes slipping away like sand through her fingers, each one precious, irreplaceable. Her thoughts raced to William, imagining him tied up to a pole in some dusty, damp warehouse, wondering what would happen to him.

"Got it!" Frieda announced triumphantly. The engine sputtered back to life. Muriel released the breath she hadn't realized she'd been holding.

"Good work," Mabel chimed from where she kept watch, her eyes scanning the dark horizon for signs of trouble.

They continued on, the boat now a steady thrum beneath them, slicing through the water with renewed vigor. But the sea was a fickle mistress, and soon a dense fog rolled over the surface, swallowing the moonlight and reducing their world to a mere few yards of visibility.

"Can you see anything?" Muriel asked, her voice barely above a whisper.

"Only shadows," Mabel replied, her own voice tinged with unease. "We'll have to slow down."

"We do not have the luxury of time," Muriel countered, she shook her hands out in an effort to relieve the tension. She eased off the throttle, her instincts agreeing despite her impatience.

"Trust your instincts, Muriel," Frieda encouraged. "We are all counting on you."

And trust she did, navigating by intuition more than sight, the rhythm of the waves a guide that seemed to whisper William's name with every crest.

Then, out of the mist, a shape loomed—a fishing skiff, adrift and abandoned. Suspicious? Perhaps. An obstacle? Definitely. Muriel veered sharply, avoiding a collision by mere inches, her heart pounding against her ribs.

"Keep an eye out," she instructed, her voice steady even as fear nipped at her resolve. "It seems we are not alone out here."

"Always," Frieda murmured, her gaze fixed on the murky waters behind them.

"Could be smugglers," Mabel offered, her words carrying the weight of unspoken dangers.

"Or worse," Muriel acknowledged, thinking of the many tales whispered in the taverns of Key West, stories of men lost to the sea—or to greed.

They sailed on, the silence among them filled with the sound puff and chug of the engine. Muriel's mind wandered to

William yet again, to the strong planes of his face, the gentle cadence of his Bahamian lilt. It was love that had brought her to this moment, love that would carry her through.

"Almost there," Mabel announced sensing the shore and then seeing it through the fog, breaking into Muriel's reverie. The outline of another island took shape through the fog, a beacon of hope in the gloom.

"Stay sharp," Frieda cautioned. "This is where it gets tricky." Each of them was an old hand at navigating these waters. The fog may have thrown off their calculations, but if they had timed it correctly, then the bit of sand ahead was the place they were looking for.

Muriel nodded, squaring her shoulders. Despite fear clinging to her like damp air, determination and the knowledge that each boat length forward brought her closer to William drove her on.

"Let us bring him home," she said, her voice imbued with a strength she drew from the depth of her affection for William, a strength that would see them through the darkness and beyond. Fortunately, the fog parted the closer they got to the little island.

⁂

As the wooden motorboat slipped through the waters, Muriel's grip on the small rudder tightened a bit more. About two hundred feet from shore, they cut the motor and used paddles to move forward. The moon—a slender crescent—hung low in the sky, a chaperone to their clandestine affair with fate. Frieda and Mabel flanked Muriel, each woman's features etched with the same silent pledge.

"Remember, timing is our dance partner tonight," Frieda whispered, her eyes scanning the dark horizon where sea met sky in an indistinguishable line of obsidian mystery. They had turned off their lanterns before reaching shore to give their eyes time to adjust to the darkness.

"Like we practiced," Mabel affirmed, checking the contents of her satchel by feel one last time. Maps, a compass, and—for luck—the carefully wrapped locket that William had given Muriel. She did not want to wear it around her neck for fear that a stray beam of light would give them away. Each item carried the weight of hope.

Muriel nodded, her thoughts flitting between the urgency of the moment and the tender memories of William's embrace. The scent of salt and freedom mingled in the air, a heady perfume for their audacious escapade. "We will make it work," she said, more to herself than to her companions.

The silenced motorboat approached a secluded inlet, its entrance guarded by gnarled mangroves whispering secrets to the night. This was where they would disembark.

"Steady now," Mabel instructed softly, using her paddle to guide the vessel toward the shadowy embrace of the shoreline. The gentle scrape of wood on sand signaled their arrival, sending a shiver of anticipation down Muriel's spine.

"Once we are through this line of trees," Muriel murmured, "it's a straight path to the warehouse."

"Let us not dilly-dally, then," Frieda said, stepping out with a splash. Together, the three women secured the boat and gathered their scant belongings.

The plan they had crafted was now a living thing, pulsing with the potential of triumph or heartbreak.

"Lead on, Captain," Frieda teased gently, her use of Muriel's unofficial title a testament to the trust they placed in her leadership.

With a nod, Muriel led the way, her mind racing with the multitude of outcomes that lay before them. Each rustle of leaves in the breeze, every snap of a twig underfoot, heightened the sense of urgency that propelled them forward. The island held its breath, waiting for the resolution of their daring endeavor.

"Almost there," Muriel repeated, though whether it was to reassure her companions or herself was unclear. They crested a small sand hill and beheld a wooden building with a large, open doorway. Lanterns flickered every fifteen feet inside the cavernous interior. There were boats in various stages of destruction, but no one seemed to be about. No night birds called. The area was oddly quiet for a tropical island.

"Ready yourselves, ladies," Muriel said, her voice steady despite the tremor of excitement that ran through her. "Let us see what we can find."

CHAPTER 11

Muriel stood outside the warehouse. The night air was thick with anticipation. She eyed the small window near the roof, her entry point for the covert rescue mission.

The girls wished Muriel luck before disappearing into the darkness to create their assigned distractions. Now, alone with her racing thoughts, she steeled her nerves. She had to get William back, propriety be damned.

Silently, Muriel shimmied up a stack of empty crates to reach the window. She slid it open and slipped inside, crouching low as her eyes adjusted to the gloomy interior. She could make out the hulking shapes of boxes and barrels. Somewhere ahead, William waited.

Step by careful step, she crept through the warehouse, senses heightened for any sign of the guards. She paused at a battered door, steadying her breathing. This was it—the moment she had been waiting for since William's capture.

Come hell or high water, they would be together again soon. She just had to have faith.

Muriel turned the doorknob, wincing as it let out a faint creak. She peered inside. A lone figure slumped in a chair beneath a flickering gas lamp. William.

Her breath caught at the sight of him. His torn clothing and bruised skin caught her attention. But he was alive. That was all that mattered now.

Muriel rushed to his side and dropped to her knees. "William," she whispered, cupping his battered face in her hands. His eyes fluttered open, and he stared at her, dazed.

"You came for me," he croaked. Despite everything, a hint of his boyish grin appeared.

"Of course I did," Muriel murmured. She reached into a side pocket where she had secured a knife to cut through his bindings. "I'll always come for you."

William flexed his sore arms with relief. "My fearless rescuer." He drew her into a desperate embrace. For a moment, they clung together, the rest of the world forgotten.

But they couldn't linger. The danger was not over yet. Muriel helped William to his feet. "Can you walk?"

He nodded. "Lead the way."

Hand in hand, they slipped from the room. Despite the flickering lantern, the warehouse still held pockets of darkness that loomed ahead. But with William at her side, Muriel was ready to face whatever came next. They would make it through this long night together.

Muriel and William moved through the shadows of the warehouse, hyper aware of any sound or movement indicating the pirates' presence. Though she longed to speak with William, to ensure he was alright, Muriel knew they must get to safety first. Somehow, she had gotten turned around. The way ahead did not look familiar. Not knowing what else to do, she just pressed on hoping to find the way she had come in.

As they reached the junction of two corridors, Muriel paused, listening. Somewhere ahead, raucous laughter and shouts drifted through the musty air. The pirates were close. She tightened her grip on William's hand, meeting his eyes. He gave a small, brave smile. They would have to be swift and clever to avoid confrontation.

Pressing against the wall, Muriel inched forward, peering around the corner. A group of scruffy pirates sat around a table, gambling, and drinking. She gestured for William to follow as she crept along the adjacent wall, moving out of their line of sight. Moving cautiously, they progressed through the maze of the warehouse.

A loud clatter made them freeze. Muriel's heart seized. But the pirates just laughed, oblivious to the escaping prisoners nearby. After an agonizing moment, she tugged William's hand, and they continued on.

The small window through which Muriel had entered came into view ahead. She was surprised and delighted to find it. Hope surged within her. They were so close now. She scrambled up and through the opening, landing outside with William following closely behind her. One more obstacle behind them.

Once outside, Muriel took William's face in her hands. "We are going to get through this," she promised, finally able to at least whisper.

He covered her hands with his own and brought them for a quick kiss. "Together," he agreed. Now to reach the motorboat.

Muriel and William sprinted through the shadows, making their way toward the docks. The night air was thick with tension as they strained their ears for any sounds of pursuit.

Suddenly, William pulled Muriel behind a stack of crates. Voices drifted from nearby as a group of pirates emerged to patrol the area. Muriel clutched William's arm, not daring to breathe. The pirates swaggered by, oblivious to the two hidden figures.

Muriel met William's eyes, seeing her own fear reflected there. But there was determination too. They had come too far to fail now.

As soon as the pirates moved out of sight, Muriel and William were up and running again. The motorboat was just ahead when a shout rang out behind them. Someone had discovered William's escape!

"Faster!" Muriel cried. Adrenaline pushed them onward as angry yells and pounding footsteps followed. The pirates were giving chase now, almost upon them.

The boat was just steps away. With a final desperate burst of speed, Muriel and William sprinted onto the little beach. The small boat waited—their salvation. They pushed the boat off the sand and leaped on board. Muriel quickly pumped the steam lever and miraculously the motor coughed and puffed to life. As they pulled away, a loud crackling noise came from the warehouse and sparks flew through the air. A column of flames shot into the sky. Each pirate turned and ran back toward the warehouse. They seemed to be more concerned with saving their loot than with recovering their prisoner.

Muriel and William sagged in relief and exhaustion. Gazing back at the retreating pirates, Muriel let out a slightly crazed laugh. They had done it. They were free. Out of the shadows and on the brightening shore appeared the two figures that Muriel had been scanning for in the darkness. She moved the boat closer to the shore to pick up her two comrades, laughing in relief and triumph.

WHERE TRADE WINDS MEET

Mabel took the boat's rudder. She pressed the lever up and down to get more air into the boiler for maximum speed. Frieda sat next to her, facing forward to give the love birds a bit of privacy for their reunion. Muriel and William clung to each other, overwhelmed with emotion. Relief washed over them in waves as the danger faded into the distance.

Muriel buried her face in William's shoulder, tears of joy and adrenaline mixing in her cheeks. "I cannot believe we actually did it," she whispered.

William stroked her hair, his own heart pounding wildly. "You three make quite a team," he said with a shaky laugh.

They had dared against all odds and societal norms, risking everything for the sake of love and friendship. And now here they were, speeding off into an uncertain future.

Muriel lifted her head to look into William's eyes. In them, she saw the same exhilaration and devotion that flooded her own spirit. No matter what happened next, they would face it together.

"I love you," she said, the depth of her feelings ringing in every word. "No pirate or disapproving parent can ever tear us apart now."

William cupped her face in his hands. "I love you. Always." He kissed her tenderly as the boat skimmed over the moonlit waves.

Muriel rested her head on William's shoulder as they headed back to Key West, the night breeze blowing her hair. She interlaced her fingers with his, drawing strength from his solid presence. After everything they had endured, just being able to sit here together seemed a miracle.

Mabel and Frieda began talking about their part of the escape plan, handing William food and a container of water. He looked ragged. Fortunately, Frieda had remembered to grab an extra set of clothes from her father's store for him to change into when they reached shore. Meanwhile, he and Muriel just clung to each other, then drifted off to sleep while Frieda and Mabel quietly whispered together, reliving their extraordinary feat.

When the lights of Key West came into view, Muriel felt a twinge of anxiety pierce her heart. She knew they still faced opposition to their relationship from her family and society at large. She squeezed William's hand, reminding herself that their love had already conquered so much.

William sensed her trepidation. "No matter what happens, I am here," he murmured. "I will always be by your side."

Muriel nodded, comforted by his words. She anticipated her parents outrage when she returned with William. They did not believe the Spanish Conch should intermingle with the British Bahamians. But she did not care about status or money. To her, he was the man who made her feel truly alive.

The boat bumped against the dock. Taking a deep breath, Muriel stood up with William's help. She raised her chin determinedly. Let them judge and scorn all they wanted. She and William would simply build a new life, one where their love was free.

As they walked down the dock hand in hand, Muriel glimpsed her brother Bryan waiting on the shore. She steeled herself for his reaction, but as they drew closer, she saw only relief on his face.

WHERE TRADE WINDS MEET

"Thank God you are safe," he said, pulling Muriel into a tight hug. She blinked back tears, overwhelmed by her brother's acceptance. With his support, her parents would come around too. Either way, she and William were ready to fight for their future.

CHAPTER 12

The following week Muriel stood at the edge of the bustling dock, the scent of salt and fish mingling with the warm breeze. She had neatly pinned up her light-brown hair, but a few rebellious strands still danced around her face. She watched as the SS *Mascotte* cut through the cerulean waves, its arrival as punctual as the tides. Among the crew disembarking the ship, she sought one familiar figure—a man whose medium build belied his steadfast presence. They had both been quite busy since their second daring rescue. William had spoken to the coastal authorities about Albert Pinder and then was immediately rushed off on a short voyage to Tampa for his company. Now he was back, and they could implement the next phase of their whispered plan into action.

"William!" Muriel called out, then pressed her lips together to stifle the tremor in her voice. Her blue eyes fixed on the second officer who turned toward her with a look of mild surprise.

"Miss Russell," William greeted, tipping his hat, his light-brown hair catching the sun's golden-hour glow. "What brings you to the docks today?"

"Have you finished your business with the coastal authorities regarding Albert Pinder?"

"Yes, they have issued a warrant for his arrest and sent his information by telephone to the various law enforcement agencies within the islands and up into the rest of Florida,"

William replied stiffly. He just had not believed that Albert had such a murderous streak to him. He had chalked up the childish behavior Albert displayed when they first met to his youth and infatuation with an unavailable woman.

"Sadly, Albert has always been a little peculiar. I am upset and disheartened for his parents. They may have old-fashioned notions about marriage, but they should not have a son who would dishonor them so." Muriel shook her head in wonder.

"I see." He smiled as her generous heart showed through in those words.

Muriel hesitated, feeling the weight of her decision. "I need to speak with you, privately," she said, hoping her lightly tanned skin did not betray the flush of anxiety beneath. She looked around to ensure no one near could overhear their conversation.

"Of course." William's gray eyes searched hers, remembering the whispered conversation on the boat after his last rescue.

"Would you come to my family's home?" she asked, each word measured. "There's something important we must discuss."

William understood the implications. "I will follow your lead," he replied, a gentle firmness in his voice. Theirs was ever the outward appearance of propriety to anyone watching their exchange.

Together, they walked from the docks, weaving through the streets of Key West. The town was alight with the laughter of children and the clatter of horse-drawn carriages, all oblivious to the silent drama anticipated by the two figures making their way through the evening din.

WHERE TRADE WINDS MEET

They arrived at the Russell residence, a modest but well-cared-for abode, its porch wrapped in the sweet embrace of bougainvillea. Muriel's hand shook ever so slightly as she turned the doorknob, the metal cold and unyielding against her skin.

"Are you certain about this, Muriel?" William's voice was low, his accent carrying a hint of the Bahamas that reminded her of distant shores and the dreams they shared in secret.

"More than anything," she assured him, pushing the door open. Her heart pounded against her ribs like the surf against the sand, each beat echoing her resolve.

Crossing the threshold, they stepped into the quiet parlor, where the setting sun cast long shadows across the floorboards. This room, which had once felt so familiar, now held the electric charge of impending revelation.

"Whatever comes," William said, taking a breath as if bracing against a gale, "I am here beside you." His hand found hers, a silent pact between them.

"Thank you," Muriel whispered, grateful for his strength. They stood side by side, united in purpose, ready to face whatever tides may come.

Muriel led William into the living room, her palm damp against his as she guided him forward. The floorboards creaked beneath their steps, a quiet chorus to the hum of conversation that filled the space. Her parents and younger brother, Bryan, basked in the warm glow of the oil lamps, their faces radiating the tranquility of the day's end.

"Mother, Father," Muriel began, her voice steady despite the quiver that threatened the edges of her words. "Bryan, this is William Albert Roberts. He is the second officer on the

SS *Mascotte* and his family is from New Providence in the Bahamas and, yes, they are British Bahamians."

Her mother looked up from her needlework. The gentle smile upon her lips did not reach her eyes. Her father's brow was etched with lines of concern that deepened as he set aside his newspaper. Young Bryan, still in the throes of adolescence, peered at them both with curiosity from behind a book about the great explorers.

No one moved or said a word except Bryan who coughed to quickly hide his mirth.

"We have something important we would like to discuss," Muriel urged, taking a position beside William, who stood with a quiet dignity, the ocean's depth reflected in his gray eyes.

The silence in the room was deafening. The soft ticking of the grandfather clock amplified the weight of the moment. Muriel glanced at William, finding courage in his supportive gaze before turning back to face her kin.

"William and I have come to tell you ... to share with you, our intentions." She took a deep breath, her chest rising with the tide of confession. "We have fallen deeply in love with one another."

Her words hung in the air, a daring seagull riding the winds of change. The rhythm of the clock seemed to skip a beat and, for a fleeting moment, the world outside—with its rigid expectations and social proprieties—faded away, leaving only the truth of two hearts entwined.

"And we wish to be together," William added, his voice resonating with a sailor's fortitude, an echo of his life at sea. His hand tightened around Muriel's, anchoring her in the swell of emotions that threatened to capsize their resolve.

WHERE TRADE WINDS MEET

Muriel's gaze swept across her family; each member was wrapped in their own silent contemplation. Her father's mouth opened and then closed, a ship adrift before finding its course. Her mother's hands were still, her needle paused mid-stitch as if caught in the fabric of time itself. And young Bryan, his explorer's heart racing with the thrill of undiscovered lands, watched them with wide, unblinking eyes.

"Love," Muriel continued, the word tasting of salt and freedom on her lips, "is the compass by which we wish to navigate our future, regardless of the storms we may face."

The ticking of the grandfather clock, which had always been a comforting constant in the Russell household, now seemed to underscore the silence that enveloped the room. Muriel felt the weight of her family's gaze, heavy as the humid air that blanketed Key West in the throes of summer. Her mother clutched at her sewing, the needle dangling like a pendulum, while her father's eyes narrowed, their gray depths stormy with brewing thoughts.

Bryan, ever the embodiment of boyish wonder, leaned forward in his seat, elbows resting on knees. His blue eyes sparkled with the sheen of intrigue, a stark contrast to the creases of concern etched upon his parents' foreheads.

"Love," Muriel whispered again, as if the word could bridge the chasm of shock.

It was Mr. Russell who found his voice first, breaking through the stillness as he rose from his armchair. "Muriel, my dear," he began, his tone betraying the mix of affection and trepidation that only a father's heart could harbor. "This news you have sprung upon us ...." He paused, searching for the right words among the swells of his own disquiet.

"William is a good man," Muriel interjected.

"Perhaps," Mr. Russell conceded, his gaze flitting from his daughter to the young man beside her. "But love, strong as it may be, cannot always weather the tides of society's judgment." His hand swept through the air, as if dispelling a wisp of cigar smoke—a motion Muriel recognized from countless evenings spent discussing the day's work at the factory.

"Your worlds are oceans apart," he continued, his voice steady but lined with the weariness of experience. "You hail from different shores, my girl. The currents of class and expectation run deep, and they can drown even the most fervent of loves."

"Father, I know the sea you speak of," Muriel replied, lifting her chin, her blue eyes unwavering. "But we have set our course together, and we shall navigate it side by side."

Mr. Russell let out a slow breath, the sound mingling with the rhythmic hum of the ceiling fan above. "And what of the storms you will face? The reefs unseen beneath the surface?"

"Every ship risks the rocks, Father," she said, her resolve buoyed by the strength of her own convictions. "But braving the unknown is the very essence of adventure."

The room held its breath, waiting for the patriarch to chart the path forward. Would he raise the flag of approval or signal for them to batten down the hatches against a love deemed too perilous to pursue?

The stillness in the parlor was as thick as the humid air outside, broken only by the faint rustle of palm fronds against the window pane. Mrs. Russell, seated in her favorite armchair with its floral upholstery, now appeared less cheery than usual.

WHERE TRADE WINDS MEET

She clasped and unclasped her hands in her lap—a silent symphony of maternal concern.

"Darling," she began, her voice carrying the weight of a mother's love mingled with the ache of hard truths. "I will not pretend I do not understand the depths of your affections, but there is a world beyond these walls that may not be as forgiving." She paused, glancing over at the young man who stood beside her daughter, an outsider to their family portrait but clearly holding a piece of Muriel's heart within his own. "The tongues of this town wag without mercy, and the labels they affix can be as binding as chains."

Muriel reached for her mother's hand, squeezing it gently. "I know, Mother," she whispered, her gaze steady even as her heart galloped within her chest.

"Reputation is a fragile bird," Mrs. Russell continued, her blue eyes reflecting the same hues of doubt and hope that danced across the waters of Key West. "Once wounded, it rarely takes flight the same way again. And you, my child, have always soared so high."

It was then that William stepped forward. His gray eyes, often cool like the morning mists of Nassau, now burned with a quiet fire. He cleared his throat. When he spoke, his voice carried the melodic lilt of the islands, underscored with a determination as solid as the lighthouse that guided seafarers home.

"Mr. and Mrs. Russell," he said, addressing them directly with a deference that belied his position as second officer aboard the SS *Mascotte*. "I stand before you, not blind to the challenges we will face, nor deaf to the whispers of society that might seek to divide us."

Muriel felt the resonance of his words bolster her spirit, even as her parents listened, weighing the sincerity of his pledge.

"Your daughter," William continued, his gaze never leaving Muriel's, "has shown me a strength and grace that surpasses any tempest I have encountered at sea. It is with that same courage that I vow to honor and cherish her, to weather any storm that might rise against us."

Muriel's heart swelled within her chest, the confirmation of their shared resolve soothing the unspoken fears that prickled beneath her skin.

"Mrs. Russell, with all due respect, I love your daughter—more deeply than the ocean's fathoms. I promise to dedicate every breath in my being to bringing joy to her life and upholding her name with the dignity it deserves."

Amid their tightly woven historical tapestry of gender roles and societal expectations, William's declaration shone like a beacon of modernity, challenging the very fabric of their long-standing traditions.

Mrs. Russell, her eyes glistening with the onset of tears that threatened to breach their banks, nodded slowly. She felt a profound sense of respect and admiration as she observed his earnest plea, realizing the genuine nature of his intentions.

Silence hung in the room like a heavy fog after William's heartfelt declaration. The ticking of the grandfather clock was the only sound that dared to pierce the quiet. Each tick was a measured step toward an uncertain future. Muriel stood beside William, her fingers interlaced with his, both sets of knuckles white with the grip of conviction.

WHERE TRADE WINDS MEET

Then a chair scraped against the wooden floor, the abruptness of the sound commanding attention. All eyes turned toward the youngest Russell, Bryan, as he rose from his seat. His blue eyes, so much like Muriel's, held a spark of youthful audacity.

With a voice stronger than anyone might have expected from his slight figure, he began. "Mother, Father, I have known William here longer than any of you. He has shown me the ropes I never learned in school—about life on the sea, about integrity. And if he says he loves Muriel, then by all the stars above, I believe him."

A murmur rippled through the room, and for a moment, it appeared the Atlantic itself had breezed through the parlor, softening the stiff collars and rigid postures of the elders present.

"Love is not something we should stifle because the town gossips will wag their tongues," Bryan continued, his light-brown hair catching the lamplight as he shook his head emphatically. "If Muriel's happy with William, then what else really matters?"

The air in the room shifted subtly, as if the young man's words had unlocked a window to let in the gentle Key West breeze. Mr. and Mrs. Russell exchanged glances, the lines of worry on their faces becoming less severe as they observed the couple before them.

Muriel felt a loosening in her chest as with the release of a long-held breath. Beside her, William's posture softened, the rigidity of defense easing into a stance of quiet hope. Their hands remained joined, a tangible symbol of their united front.

"Look at them," Bryan said softly, motioning toward his sister and her suitor. "They are ready to face whatever comes. Should we be standing with them, rather than adding to the weight they have already chosen to carry?"

The room was now awash in contemplation, the storm of opposition waning into a contemplative calm. There was an unspoken understanding that the love between Muriel and William was a force unto itself, one that could very well withstand the shifting sands of societal expectation.

Mrs. Russell, her earlier reservations still lingering like the scent of jasmine after dusk, allowed herself a small smile, the kind that acknowledged the bravery inherent in true love. Mr. Russell, too, seemed to reassess the situation. His furrowed brow smoothed as the reality of his children's words settled over him like the warmth of the Florida sun.

As the tension ebbed, leaving in its wake the possibility of acceptance and the promise of support, Muriel felt the room breathe with them. It seemed to embrace the notion that sometimes the heart's compass was the truest guide through life's tumultuous waters.

Charles Zelana Russell, a man whose life had been as much shaped by the tobacco leaves he rolled as boy and who had been bound all his life by the traditions of Key West society, shared a glance with his wife. It was the kind of look that carried years of unspoken understanding and love, a silent conversation that only two souls intertwined by time could comprehend. In that brief exchange, there was a mutual surrendering of old fears, a tentative step toward the embrace of something as unpredictable and wild as the sea itself—love without conditions.

WHERE TRADE WINDS MEET

And Susan Elizabeth Roberts Russell, with her clerk's precision for detail, noted not just the tremble in her daughter's hands but also the resolve etched in her stance. She rose from her perch on the edge of the embroidered armchair, her movements graceful despite the weight of the moment. With a few assured steps, she came to stand before Muriel, taking her daughter's hand in hers—a lifeline offered amid the storm of emotions.

"Darling," Mrs. Russell began, her voice the soft lilt of a lullaby against the howling winds of change, "you have always had a compass true to your heart. We have seen it guide you through every trial." Her blue eyes, mirrors of Muriel's own, shimmered with unshed tears. "Your father and I ... we may not have charted these waters before, but if this is the course you have set, then we will sail it with you."

"Mother ..." Muriel's voice wavered; a tender note caught in the breeze. Mrs. Russell's touch was gentle but firm, as if imparting strength through her fingertips.

"Love is a voyage, my dear. There will be storms and doldrums, but also the most breathtaking sunrises," Mrs. Russell continued, her wisdom wrapped in the warmth of acceptance. "And who are we to deny you the stars under which you wish to navigate?"

In those words, spoken with the grace of a seasoned seafarer, Muriel found an anchor in the tempest of her fears. Here, in the heart of her childhood home, with the scent of salt and cigars lingering like the memories they all held dear, the Russells banded together like the sturdy planks of a ship, ready to weather whatever the future might hold.

"William," Charles Russell began, his voice carrying the gravitas of a man who had navigated his own share of life's choppy waters, "I have seen you stand steadfast against more than just the gales at sea. You are a man of substance." He paused, his gray eyes locking onto William's. "You and Muriel are setting sail into uncharted territory. I will not pretend there are not squalls ahead, but I hope, together, you will find calmer seas."

The younger man's throat tightened as he clasped Mr. Russell's hand. "Thank you, sir. I know the waters we are venturing into are rife with unknowns, but I promise you, my devotion to Muriel is as constant as the North Star."

As their handshake broke, a weight seemed to lift from the room, making space for something new and fragile: hope. It fluttered in the hearts of everyone present like a delicate schooner, catching a favorable wind for the first time.

And then, as naturally as the tide coming in, Muriel stepped toward William. Her blue eyes, so often mirroring the vastness of the ocean that surrounded their island home, now reflected only the man before her. Without a word, she wrapped her arms around him. It was an embrace that told of storms weathered and a future embraced; it spoke of love's victory over the rigid mores of their era.

"Look at them, Charles," Mrs. Russell whispered to her husband, a warm smile touching her lips. "They remind me of us at their age—undaunted, even by the fiercest gale."

"Indeed, Susan," he replied, his voice a quiet rumble of agreement. "It seems love's current is too strong for any barrier we or society might put in its way."

WHERE TRADE WINDS MEET

In each other's arms, William and Muriel shared laughter that danced through the room, lighthearted as a seabird on the wing. It was the sound of chains breaking, of horizons widening. They stood together, not as two people defying the world, but as two souls united in the certainty that their journey was just beginning, with every sunrise promising a day less bound by yesterday's expectations.

"Let the town talk," murmured William, his breath warm against Muriel's ear. "We will write our own story, one sunrise at a time."

About the Author

Hello, My name is L.J. Green. If you really must know that stands for Lillian Jade Green. I am a newly penned author recounting the tales of my late, great aunt and cousin who were quite the black sheep of the family I must tell you. I had just graduated from high school when our nation was fully involved in some horrific and trying times. With nothing better to do I went to clean out our attic and I found some old diaries. They were tucked away in an old steamer trunk that my mother had inherited from her mother. My own mother was never interested in the contents as they looked to be well-preserved and undisturbed for quite a number of years. I truly enjoyed reading them during that long, hot summer when we had very little money for frills of any kind and no prospects for that changing any time in the future.

Having enjoyed them I thought I would turn them into a fiction series for you to enjoy as well. The adventures that follow are almost entirely recounted as written with just a flourish or two of my own. I hope you will enjoy them as much as I have in reading and recounting them.

Read more at https://authorlillianjgreen.blogspot.com/.

Connect With the Author

Website: https://authorlillianjgreen.blogspot.com
Email: lillianJGreen1900s@gmail.com
Author Facebook: https://www.facebook.com/Author.LJGreen/
Series Facebook: https://www.facebook.com/MisadventuresJanieAndDiane
Threads: https://threads.net/@authorljgreen
Instagram: https://www.instagram.com/authorljgreen/
TikTok: https://www.tiktok.com/@authorljgreen
Pinterest: https://www.pinterest.com/LJGreensEmporium/
YouTube Channel: https://www.youtube.com/@AuthorLJGreen
Goodreads: https://www.goodreads.com/author/show/23094591.L_J_Green
Bookbub: https://www.bookbub.com/authors/l-j-green
Amazon Author Profile Page: https://www.amazon.com/author/ljgreen
My LinkTree: https://ljgreenauthor.my.canva.site/

Also by LJ Green

Misadventures of Janie and Diane
A Widow's Dilemma in Cuba - An in between novella

Standalone
Where Trade Winds Meet

Watch for more at https://authorlillianjgreen.blogspot.com/.

About the Publisher

Welcome future writers and current authors to our Southern Dragon Publishing company website. We will be adding information, resources, tips, and tricks for those who wish to publish and market their stories. Our services categories are below. We have detailed information about each service and a pricing schedule on separate pages. We look forward to helping you on your self-publishing journey.

https://SouthernDragonPublishing.com

Milton Keynes UK
Ingram Content Group UK Ltd.
UKHW020133021224
451791UK00018B/71/J

9 781961 386167